T0369310

Praise for Pramoedya Ananta Toer

"Pramoedya Ananta Toer should get the Nobel Prize."

—Carolyn See, *The Washington Post*

"Like Steinbeck, he traces history through the lives of people who till the soil, who wander barefoot onto third-class trains."

—*The New York Times Book Review*

"Reading the book, one is reminded in many respects of John Steinbeck. . . . Pramoedya is concerned with the same interplays of the human condition, of sorrow and injustice, of the dreams of men that either never fulfill themselves or come true at the expense of a terrible price . . . gripping, haunts the memory."

—Martin Booth, *The Washington Post Book World*

"Toer's creative energy and fervent humanitarianism earn him a place alongside Malraux and Steinbeck." —*Kirkus Reviews*

"Here is an author half a world away from us whose art and humanity are both so great that we instantly feel we've known him—and he us—all our lives." —*USA Today*

"As eloquent and sensual as James Baldwin. As hip and smart and bleak and dark as Dashiell Hammet. A novelist who should get in line for the Nobel Prize." —*Los Angeles Times*

"Pramoedya Ananta Toer has lived the life of an Indonesian Solzhenitsyn. His prose is evocative, almost intoxicating."

—Mark Pinksy, *Los Angeles Times*

"Pramoedya Ananta Toer is Indonesia's Albert Camus. The comparison works on many levels, not the least of which is the author's ability to confront monumental questions on their most elemental plains."

—*San Francisco Chronicle*

"Electrifying . . . The prose is lyrical, musical, yet as hard as shrapnel." —*Publishers Weekly*

"Pramoedya Ananta Toer hardly has an equal in South-East Asia. Few could match his stature, insight, intellectual acumen, and the sublime power of his deceptively simple prose." —*The Independent*

Praise for Pramoedya Ananta Toer

PENGUIN BOOKS

IT'S NOT AN ALL NIGHT FAIR

PRAMOEDYA ANANTA TOER (1925–2006) was born on the island of Java. He was imprisoned first by the Dutch from 1947 to 1949 for his role in the Indonesian revolution, then by the Indonesian government as a political prisoner. Many of his works have been written while he was in prison, including the Buru Quartet, which was conceived in stories the author told to other prisoners during his confinement on Buru Island from 1969 to 1979. Pramoedya is the author of thirty works of fiction and nonfiction. His novels have been translated into twenty languages. He received the PEN Freedom-to-write Award in 1988 and the Ramon Magsaysay Award in 1995.

C. W. WATSON is the head of the Department of Anthropology at the University of Kent at Canterbury where he has taught for over twenty years. Prior to that he worked in universities in Malaysia and Indonesia. His latest book is *Of Self and Nation: Autobiographical Representations of Indonesia* (2001).

PRAMOEDYA
ANANTA TOER

It's Not an All Night Fair

Translated with an Introduction, Postscript, and Notes by C. W. WATSON

PENGUIN BOOKS

PENGUIN BOOKS
Published by the Penguin Group
Penguin Group (USA) Inc., 375 Hudson Street, New York, New York 10014, U.S.A.
Penguin Group (Canada), 90 Eglinton Avenue East, Suite 700, Toronto,
Ontario, Canada M4P 2Y3 (a division of Pearson Penguin Canada Inc.)
Penguin Books Ltd, 80 Strand, London WC2R 0RL, England
Penguin Ireland, 25 St Stephen's Green, Dublin 2, Ireland (a division of Penguin Books Ltd)
Penguin Group (Australia), 250 Camberwell Road, Camberwell,
Victoria 3124, Australia (a division of Pearson Australia Group Pty Ltd)
Penguin Books India Pvt Ltd, 11 Community Centre,
Panchsheel Park, New Delhi – 110 017, India
Penguin Group (NZ), cnr Airborne and Rosedale Roads, Albany,
Auckland 1310, New Zealand (a division of Pearson New Zealand Ltd)
Penguin Books (South Africa) (Pty) Ltd, 24 Sturdee Avenue,
Rosebank, Johannesburg 2196, South Africa

Penguin Books Ltd, Registered Offices:
80 Strand, London WC2R 0RL, England

Originally published in Indonesia under the title
Bukan Pasar Malam © 1951 Pramoedya Ananta Toer
The English version was first published in the United States of America
in the journal *Indonesia* No. 15 by Cornell University, April 1973
Published by Equinox Publishing (Asia) Pte. Ltd. 2001
Published in Penguin Books 2006

LIBRARY OF CONGRESS CATALOGING IN PUBLICATION DATA
Toer, Pramoedya Ananta, 1925–2006.
[Bukan pasar malam. English]
It's not an all night fair / Pramoedya Ananta Toer ; translated from the Indonesian by C. W. Watson.
p. cm.
Novel.
In English; translated from Indonesian.
Originally published in the journal: Indonesia (Ithaca, N.Y.)—Apr. 1973, no. 15.
ISBN 0 14 30.3702 1
I. Watson, C. W. II. Title.
PL5089.T8B8313 2006
899'.22132—dc22 2006044800

146119709

Content

Introduction

The generation of writers which emerged after the Second World War is known as the *Angkatan* '45 (The Generation of '45). Among students of Indonesian literature it is a commonplace that the Angkatan '45 developed a style of writing and a critical focus which differed considerably from that of their predecessors, the writers who clustered round the magazine *Pudjangga Baru*. Among the distinctive traits of post-war writing which are usually mentioned are the predominance of realism in the short story and the novel, as opposed to the romanticism and thesis novels of the earlier generation, and the development of a prose style which is noticeable for its terseness and the absence of lyricism. One also notices the use of cynicism and irony to convey oblique comments on the political situation, and an interest in sordid, squalid detail for its own sake, a *nostalgie de la boue*.

Clearly the experience of the Japanese occupation and the revolution account in large measure for the difference in outlook between the two generations, but the difference in educational and class background is also relevant. The Pudjangga Baru group consisted of those to whom the whole Dutch perspective had been open. They had a thorough Dutch education and were largely divorced from their own native society, whereas the Angkatan '45 consisted of those who had not had the opportunity of university or tertiary education of any sort and in some cases were brought up in the traditional educational milieux or in the Taman Siswa schools that had been established specifically to counter Dutch educational influence. It is hardly surprising, therefore, that what they chose to write about and the attitudes adopted in their writing differ considerably from earlier writers.

Turning from the pre-occupation novels to the works of Pramoedya Ananta Toer, the finest prose-writer of the Angkatan '45, one is immediately struck by the directness of the writing, by the involvement of the writer in what is being described. This impression is created first by the perspective from which the books are written: often the story is told in the first person, allowing a great flexibility in comment on the narrative. The story never has to be rigged so that a particular case can be made out. The themes of the story do not, as is the case in the works of the earlier generation, control the pattern of related scenes. Instead the individual observation becomes the focus of the writing, and what determines the quality of the novel is the selective vision and the organization of the descriptions.

The break from the Pudjangga Baru style is startling. The dramatic switch of forms of the novel within such a short historical period is unmatched in the history of the European novel which evolved its stylistic forms over a much longer period of time, although, according to critics such as Roland Barthes, the changes were equally dramatic. This break with the immediate past is in fact only open to a society whose literary tradition is derivative; that is, where the body of written literature has been wholly taken over from the examples of an external culture. In this situation the multiplicity of forms and styles makes the choice of a particular model to follow fairly open, although clearly socio-historical circumstances or accidents perhaps determine which models are available at particular moments. It has already been illustrated by critics how the models which the Pudjangga Baru took up are derived from the Tachtigers, the Dutch poets of the 1880's; and there are similar accounts to illustrate the intellectual stylistic debt which the Angkatan '45, in particular the poet, Chairil Anwar, owed to more contemporary European literary movements associated with Rilke and the Dutch writers Marsmann and Slauerhoff in poetry, and Hemingway and Steinbeck in prose.

What must have attracted Pramoedya to the writings of Steinback, for example, is the same kind of sympathy which the majority of readers of the realist novels of the turn of the century must have had for the writings of Dreiser, Upton Sinclair and others. This is a kind of writing which is concerned to describe the wretchedness of life as it is lived by the majority; the insecurity, the disgusting physical conditions, the misery, and bestiality to which people are reduced by their struggle and the absence of any light or joy in their lives. But beyond the mere documentation of this, there is a tremendous sympathy generated by the poignancy of the descriptions. Zola had tried to detach himself as much as possible, to put down the conditions as he saw them in the manner of a social research worker, since this appeared to him to be the first step before one could take remedial action. There had to be an objective diagnosis before the correct social medicine could be prescribed. But in the writings of the great American realists there is the immediately felt identity of the writer with the people he is describing, and it is perhaps this capacity to feel which enables him to recreate the passions and desires of the characters in his novel.

It is this clear commitment, I think, which explains the response of Pramoedya and his fellow writers to the contemporary American fiction of that era. Besides the difference in class origins of Pramoedya and the Pudjangga Baru writers which goes a long way to explaining the former's *saeva indignatio* and the compassion in his writings, the exigencies created by the occupation and the revolution had forced the intellectuals into a much closer association with their countrymen than the earlier writers ever experienced. Pramoedya's milieu, his circle of friends and his experiences were quite unlike the refined intellectual environment of Sutan Takdir Alisjahbana and his fellow writers who, although they professed a common identity with the aspirations of nationalism, were nevertheless prevented by their social position from appreciating the experiences and emotions thrown up by the revolution.

But while the range and the depth of Pramoedya's descriptive writing is clearly superior to that of the pre-1942 writers, in most of his writings he seems to have succumbed to the fate which befell many Western realist writers because of their emotional commitment to the material of their novels. The reason why one subscribes to realism as opposed to naturalism is surely because the latter is too uncritical and defines no stance in relation to the situations it describes. Naturalism is often merely an unorganized description of what occurs in reality, a straightforward reproduction of visible action. Yet literature should attempt to do more than simply reproduce. It should select, comment on and explain. This is what realism in contradiction to naturalism does, and the best examples of realism are those which are sufficiently detached to make a statement about reality which the reader is asked to endorse. The question naturalism asks is: have you seen this? No? Then I'll show it to you. Realism's question is: you've seen this, haven't you? But have you ever thought about it in this way?

In many of his novels and short stories Pramoedya seems unable to do this. In *Keluarga Gerilja* (Family of Guerrillas), his best-known novel at that time, for example, there is an unrelieved description of misery, wretchedness and futility; there seems an underlying fatalism where all one can do in a plea for an authentic kind of living is to point to the idealism (or obduracy?) of individuals who are prepared to continue to push the stone up the hill in the certain knowledge that it will come tumbling down. There seem to be few significant actions in the book, by which I mean that no action appears commendable because it offers an alternative which is more than a temporary respite to the appalling depression of the narrative. Pramoedya has nothing to offer beyond the description of what he sees and a great sympathy for the sufferers, although even this is a major achievement. Perhaps one could make the same point about Steinbeck. What is lacking is a commitment informing the work. There is a penetrating analysis of contemporary conditions but no creative synthesis in which these conditions are totalized and a meaning constructed out of the fragments.

This criticism does not, however, apply to *Bukan Pasar Malam*. In this novel there is a far greater sensitivity to contemporary issues than in Pramoedya's other works. Here for once the "camera eye" yields to the informed observer and there is a continual questioning and an attempt to reconstruct something out of apparent chaos. The book works on two complementary levels: the first is a personal account, narrated in the first person, of the encounter of a son with his dying father. This encounter, while forcing the hero to self-analysis in the face of the values and meaning of his father's life, compels him, because of his father's passionate concern with politics and the consequent vicissitudes in the fortunes of the family, to lift his analysis on to a higher more encompassing plane. From this vantage point his personal life is seen from a more transcendent perspective as being part of an existential problem with political and social parameters. And he learns that meaning is to be found only by locating one's personal life in the complex fabric of these parameters. In the process of doing this, then, norms and values are established which serve as guides for purposeful action. A particular person's life and his writing acquire significance for the future, in which one hopes to create a better life, by offering tentative solutions to problems which have now been at least partially recognized and defined.

In *Bukan Pasar Malam* Pramoedya is groping towards some sort of synthesis of experiences. While the father is dying, the hero reflects on his life trying to recall what his father tried to achieve, and he is aided in this by his friends who recount for him the significance of his father in their lives. The *dukun* (shaman) recalls the father's insistence on the need to continue to educate the children even under Dutch supervision. The sister talks about the father's attitude to the rampant opportunism which sprang up after the war. And at the meeting before the funeral where his father's friends are gathered together they discuss the father and his unbending attitude, vividly established by the story of his endurance at the card table. At the end what the hero remembers is that his father refused to make a clown of himself by engaging in the rat-race for political recognition, because for him the important decisions and complementary actions to be taken could not possibly be arrived at in the prevailing context of insincerity.

The tone and structure of the book remind me of Raymond Williams' *Border Country* where the author adopts the same structure as is used in *Bukan Pasar Malam*. Williams' hero goes back to visit his dying father and in the emotionally charged atmosphere he is forced to confront his father and lay his own values against the other's. From this personal encounter there emerges a reappraisal of values which allows the hero to set his own experience within a wider perspective. The difference between the two books, it seems to me, lies in that where Williams shies away from describing his hero's emotions—which one always feels are to him a little suspect—Pramoedya is intent on recreating the quick, immediate feelings of his hero, making his book in this respect richer than *Border Country.* (It should perhaps be mentioned in fairness to the latter that its scope is far more ambitious than Pramoedya's book and contains a more finely detailed description of the circumstances of the hero than the sketch in *Bukan Pasar Malam.*)

Bukan Pasar Malam is structured around the description of various discrete scenes each of which has a certain autonomy in that each is expressive of a particular incident which is significant for the individuals involved in it. At the same time the separate incidents are linked through the mediation of the narrator, the *aku* (I) of the novel, to his own conspectus of the reality which he sees. Thus while the reader can enjoy in their own right the accounts of the goat meat butcher on the trip to the dukun as highly illustrative and vivid cameos of the Javanese ways of life, the organizing consciousness of the narrator provides a synthesizing element which allows us to consider both as structural elements within a totality or, in different terms, as two experiences of a life-style which contribute to the narrator's awareness of himself.

This movement in the novel, first isolating experiences and then drawing them together again, can perhaps be briefly illustrated in an analysis of the following passage where the hero is talking to one of his sisters:

> "And how did you live all the time father was in prison?"
>
> She did not reply. I saw her eyes fill with tears. And a communication which was clearer than a reply was reflected in those eyes filled with tears. I didn't press her.
>
> "How did father get free from the 'reds'?"
>
> "Father was imprisoned in the jail here, then he was marched

> to Rembang. And when they got to Rembang the Siliwangi division had already begun to enter the district and father was freed. But mother's brother-in-law was killed here."
>
> "Yes. War's really a curse for men," I said, comforting her. "War forces man to examine himself. Because, little sister, in one's self there lies everything there is in the world, and everyone else feels this is so, too."
>
> I faltered. My words were really intended for myself and were not meant for my sister at all.

The narrator is trying to elicit from his sister an account of what happened to the family during the fighting, and gradually through his sister's hesitations and the pain which the memory brings with it, the account is pieced together; the father was imprisoned and taken to another district and then freed, but another relative died. But while the incidents are recounted we are reminded of the lived experience of the events by the two sentences: "I saw her eyes fill with tears. And a communication which was clearer than a reply was reflected in those eyes filled with tears." So while working at the level of simple narrative description of the past, the writing by its focus on the subjective attitude to this experience suggests the significance of the related facts to the people involved; and at the same time the narrator is seen to comprehend at three distinct levels. He takes in the information about what has happened; he understands what his sister felt at the time and what the family must have gone through, and he understands the feelings of his sister now when she thinks back on the past. For this reason he does not press her for a more explicit account.

The words of comfort which he addresses to his sister are, as he points out, intended mainly for himself. The content of what he says, the generalization about war and personal experience, indicate a tentative step toward the search for meaningfulness. Out of the agglomeration of experiences he tries to find something of universal significance to make the whole explicable. Throughout the novel he is trying to make this leap to transcendence. As the incidents in the novel follow in succession he tries to weld them together and provide some sort of tenable cohesiveness, even though the statements sometimes risk appearing insubstantial and suspiciously metaphysical.

It should be apparent from what has been said that I regard *Bukan Pasar Malam* as in the best realist tradition and comparable to Western novels within this tradition. This translation is therefore intended not simply to acquaint the non-Indonesian reader with a good example of Indonesian literature but to offer the book for consideration as a work of literature without further qualification.

Although I have tried to be as literal as possible in the translation, I have been most concerned with trying to convey the nuances and the connotations of the Indonesian and this sometimes required periphrasis in English.

C. W. WATSON
University of Hull, England, 1972

It's Not an All Night Fair

I

In fact the letter wouldn't have been so distressing, if only I hadn't previously sent a letter whose content didn't make pleasant reading. This is the letter which I received:

Blora, 17 December 1949

"My dear son,

There is no greater joy on this earth than the pleasure of a father getting his son back again, his eldest son, the bearer of his father's honor and pride, a son who for some time has been kept apart from the bustle of society, kept apart from normal human life.

My son,

I can imagine your inner anguish, I can imagine your suffering in a cramped cell, because I myself have gone through it at a time of the P . . . [1] *rebellion, for two weeks living in three jails. From that time on till today every night I have prayed to Almighty God for the safety and happiness of the whole family from generation to generation. May the sins of the whole family be forgiven by Him."*

Yes, that was the beginning of the letter which I received after I'd been out of prison two weeks. The angry letter which I'd sent and this reply which I'd received brought tears to my eyes. And I made a promise to myself: I must keep a check on what I say.

I had no idea that my father had been imprisoned by the communists, too. And six months later another letter came from Blora. This time it wasn't from my father but from an uncle.

"If you can, return to Blora for a few days. Your father's ill. At first it was malaria and coughing. Then it became worse with piles. And now it has been discovered that your father has T.B. He's in hospital now and has vomited blood four times."

At first, reading the news, I was shocked. There was a tightness in my chest. Panic followed. In my mind rose the picture: father. Then: money. Where could I get the money for the fare? This made me wander around the city of Djakarta—looking for friends and loans.

It was hot those days. And vehicles, tens of thousands of them, sprayed dust on sweating bodies. And the dust was composed of a number of things: dry snot, horse dung, bits of motor tires, bits of tires from bicycles and *betjak*[2] and perhaps also bits of tires of my own bicycle which the other day slipped along the roads which I was now passing. And this dust of many kinds stuck, with the sweat, like glue to the body. This made me swear a little—just a little—to myself.

Supposing I had a car—just supposing, I said—all this might not be happening. Then I also thought that people who do have a car cause a lot of trouble to those who don't. And they don't realize it.

Within an hour after *magrib*[3] I was successful in getting myself into debt. If my good friend had not been able to hand me his money while saying *you can use this money for the time being,* my situation would certainly have been more agonizing than just now. The angry letter which I had sent earlier had resulted in feelings of guilt lying heavy on my chest. And in order to remove these feelings I was obliged to go and meet my father who was now ill. This is what I said to myself.

Between the darkness and last crimson rays in the west my bicycle slipped along the small road in front of the palace. The palace—bathed in electric light. God knows how many thousands of watts. I didn't know. I calculated along these lines: the electricity in the palace is at least five kilowatts. And supposing it wasn't enough, someone just had to take up a telephone, and the palace would get more.

The President, of course, was a practical man—not like those who struggled for life at the side of the road day after day. If you're not the President or a minister and you want to get an increase of electricity, thirty or fifty watts, you have to have the nerve to give two or three hundred rupiah in the way of a bribe. It really isn't practical. And if the people in the palace want to go to A or to B everything is in readiness—planes, cars, cigarettes and money. And just to get to Blora I have to first go around Djakarta and contract a debt. A life like that's really not practical.

And if you become President and your mother's ill or suppose it's your father or someone from your close family—tomorrow or the next day you can visit them. And supposing you're a minor official whose salary is only enough to allow you to go on breathing, even asking for leave to go is difficult. Because the petty heads of offices feel big if they can deny their staffs something.

All of this simply expressed the resentment in my heart. Democracy really is a beautiful system. You are allowed to become President. You are allowed to choose the job you like. You have the same rights as everyone else. And it's democracy which makes it so that I don't need to *sembah*[4] or bow to the President or ministers or other important people. Honestly, this, too, is one of democracy's victories. And you are allowed to do whatever you want, provided that it's within the sphere of the law. But if you don't have money, you will be so paralyzed, you won't be able to move. In a democratic country you're allowed to buy whatever you like. But if you don't have money, you're only allowed to look at those goods you'd like to have. This too is a kind of victory for democracy.

All this filled my thoughts while I was pedaling with the borrowed money in my pocket. And, yes, even a loan is an act of generosity or even of humanity when times are tight.

Debts! Presidents! Ministers! Excellencies! And diseases! Cars! Sweat and dust of horse dung!—My heart cried out.

2

Early in the morning the first train had already rolled out on its track from Gambir station. The high mound of red earth which I always used to see in the Japanese period whenever I went to Blora now stood there only a quarter of its size. It had been washed down by the rains. Dug up. Swept away by the rains. Suddenly I shuddered seeing the mound of red earth in the station at Djatinegara. Was not the life of men every day dug up, washed down, and swept away, too, like that mound of red earth?

That morning a thin mist still curtained my view. And I dragged my gaze away from the window—so as not to see the mound of earth. What came into my mind was father. Was not my father's life also dug up, washed down, and swept away, too? And because I had a wife, and my wife was sitting beside me, I looked across at her. I said:

"We're not going for a honeymoon. What we're doing now is going on a pilgrimage to a man who's sick."

The rattle and roar of the train which was beginning to move off again made it so I couldn't hear what she said. I could only see her mouth mumbling. And I said again:

"Tomorrow at twelve noon we'll be in Blora."

I saw her nod. Then again I looked out of the train. The morning mist, as time went by, grew thinner. Then Klender, too, became visible from the train window. The skeletons of armored cars, bren carriers and trucks lay sprawled out in the fields and at the side of the road—English guns that had been put out of action by the corps of *pemuda*[1], and also put out of action by their own leaders. And I remembered all of a sudden: the troops of pemuda who were so hard pressed by the wealth of artillery of the foreign troops that eventually they crossed the Tjakung river.

Then the train, too, reached Tjakung. There were a lot of my memories bound up with that little village. Tjakung—in the surrounds of the rubber plantation where one after the other the troops of pemuda and then the foreign troops had been entrapped.

I drew at a cigarette. And the chill of the morning together with the chill of the wind weren't so noticeable now. The ricefields, some fallow and some ready for harvesting, pursued each other in turn. And in the old days a Dutch Piper Cub would sometimes hurl grenades at farmers in those fields. Sometimes, too, the plane would land in the fallow fields and steal the goats of the villagers. Yes, all that came back to me now. And in those grasses too some of the comrades holding the railway line as their front had lain stretched out dead and their blood had soaked that grass which was always green.

"What time do we get to Semarang?" my wife asked.

"Four."

And I pursued by memories again. Krandji, Tambun, Tjikarang—the chain of defenses before the first military action. And the train hurried on with all its speed. And suddenly I remembered again my uncle's letter: vomited blood four times. And my memory halted and hovered around the word, blood. Then I remembered also the way the letter continued:

> *"I think your father can't be expected to recover. You can come home, can't you? Of course you can come home."*

I shivered right through my body—like having malaria. And the soldiers' one-act play disappeared from my thoughts. It was my father who was pictured again.

"Let's not stay too long in Blora," said my wife. I looked at my wife. I felt my forehead thicken with wrinkles. And I replied curtly:

"We'll see what the situation's like first." For a moment the image of my father disappeared.

"Perhaps if you stay too long, I'll be forced to come home ahead of you."

I was annoyed.

She looked closely at me. Before—before we were engaged—her eyes had seemed really beautiful to me. But the beauty had gone now. Yes, her eyes were like the eyes of anybody else and didn't interest me. And I returned her gaze. Perhaps my rotten eyes[2]—and I'd known they were rotten since I was small—didn't interest her anymore either. I replied:

"That's up to you."

My head and also my eyes were withdrawn from the direction of her gaze and I looked again out of the window.

We had reached Lemah Abang now.

Momentarily, reminiscences of the old days have a soothing effect. The old days—four years ago! Without warning the Dutch had rained on our defenses from three directions with eight or ten howitzers. Their number could be calculated by the ex-artillery men of the pre-war Dutch Colonial Army. The people panicked. They ran to the ricefields, I still remembered the time, I shouted cupping my hands over my mouth: Don't run! Lie flat. But they were too many, too confused, too afraid—and they didn't hear my voice. And then I lay on my stomach under a large tree and I saw one, two, three, four, five shells from a big gun fall and explode round about the swarms of people who were fleeing. Blood, Victims, Corpses. And my memories went from blood, victims, corpses, to letter, uncle and father.

I sighed. My heart was cut through. I felt things keenly, it's true. And my family too was composed of people who felt things keenly.

I shut my eyes tight so as not to see the sight of the Lemah Abang area. But still there were pictured remnants of my memories. An extraordinary side-effect of the Dutch bombardment:

four sheep, dead in front of their pen. And something harrowing: an old sheep, pregnant, with its eyes fixed on the sky, its head resting against the support of a tethering post, its two back feet kneeling, with its front feet still standing upright—and the sheep was already dead. When I shook the sheep's body a little, it fell to the ground. It didn't move. Honestly—it was already dead. A comrade said just cut that sheep up. I looked at the eyes, staring and white. There was a shuddering in my chest. I ran back. And that image of the sheep, its eyes fixed on the sky, I carried about in my head for three days. Sheep! My memories moved on—the sheep became a man and the man was my father.

I sighed.

There was also a shudder in my chest; I moaned.

"What's the matter?" my wife asked.

"I've probably caught a chill," I replied.

"Put on your jacket."

And I now put on the jacket again which I had taken off after stowing the luggage in the rack at Gambir. At that time after getting that done I had felt too hot. The feeling of heat had been made worse by the fear that we wouldn't get seats.

She did up the buttons.

"You get a chill very easily," my wife added.

I let this reminder of hers lie.

Now my thoughts pictured the grave—mankind's final place. But sometimes mankind does not find a place in the womb of the earth. Yes, sometimes. Sailors, soldiers in wartime—frequently they don't get a final resting place. And my thoughts imagined:—supposing it was father who didn't get a place.

I shivered.

My eyes grew moist. But tears didn't fall.

"Ah, I don't want to follow through all the images in my mind." I cried to myself.

Then I thought: what if I was to win a lottery. This was a splendid daydream. And this daydream ended with the old thought: in the end man dies. Dies. Is ill. And illness brought my thoughts back to my father.

Again I sighed.

"Let's hope uncle was too hasty in writing that letter," said my wife. "Let's hope that father's condition is not so bad as it's been painted."

Again I looked at those eyes which didn't interest me very much any more. This time she lowered her eyes and touched up her hair which had been disarrayed by the wind.

"Let's hope so," I said.

I looked out of the window again. Rubber plantations followed, fast one after the other. Small towns which I often used to pass through before, I now passed through again. And scores of memories, some bitter, some pleasant, invaded my thoughts at their own will. And it was then that I realized: sometimes a man isn't strong enough to fight against his own memories. And I smiled at my realization. Yes, sometimes unconsciously man is too strong and drowns his own awareness. I smiled again.

"What's the time, *mas*?"[3] my wife asked.

My eyes looked towards her. Again my glance met with those eyes that were once pretty and which didn't interest me any more now. Just for a moment. Then I dropped my gaze to my watch. I replied:

"It's almost nine."

"Maybe the telegram has already been sent."

"Let's hope so," I said.

And I looked out of the window again. Now it was the telegram which was pictured in my thoughts. There was a possibility that the telegram, which ran, *arriving tomorrow with wife*, might act as a medicine for father. In fact that hope was no longer an original one. The night before a friend had said, *You've been in prison for a long time—two and a half years! And during that time your father must certainly have been longing for your coming home. Not only that. I'm sure he's been worrying about your situation too.* And it was that which prompted me to send—I mean told me to send—the telegram. And the same friend also said, *Go. Perhaps your coming may act as an effective medicine for him.*

Thoughts like those died suddenly the moment my eyes fell on a village in the middle of ricefields blanketed by thick bamboos and trees. I knew very well how things were in that little village. That village had been under the control of bandits. Once, I—in my company—had been on patrol there and had made a long report. And the report grew brittle in a cupboard. And I struck up a friendship with a pretty girl. Because the village was in the hands of a landlord, my thoughts came to the conclusion: she must be a half-caste. But I don't care. And her father promised me: *If you marry my daughter, sir, you won't need to work. The ricefields are plentiful enough. And sir, you can take half of my ricefields.* And I became heady at hearing this offer. At that time poverty was always flying about in the air and swooping down at my head. Yes, those days I was always smiling because of that promise. But the patrol couldn't stay longer than a night and a day. And our company went back to base.

Subsequently I went back there again. But the pretty girl had already been carried away by the bandits. And I came back with regrets and also with a feeling of pleasure because the attempt to pawn myself hadn't come off. But the beauty of the girl and her fate kept hounding me in my thoughts.

Then I spoke to myself like this:

"Now she's living comfortably with the bandit who carried her off. She's already got two children now. Her body's wrapped in silks and jewelry of gold and precious stones."

The train was traveling fast. And that village, too, was wiped away from view, from memory.

I coughed.

"You're too close to the window," said my wife.

And we changed places. I tightened the collar of my jacket around my neck. Then I lay back. Closed my eyes. Dozed. But sleep couldn't follow with its security. The train became fuller and fuller with new passengers. So I opened my eyes again. We had come to an area which had just recently been freed from the threat and terror of Darul Islam[4] and we saw bits of telegraph wire, some broken off, some sticking out of bent-over telegraph poles and straggling over the ground.

"Wah. The telegram doesn't have a chance of getting there," I said.

"Yes. The telegram doesn't have a chance of getting there," my wife agreed.

The train went on. Went on. Went on . . .

Semarang.

We stayed the night in a hotel. The hotel was incredibly dirty. But we were able to rest contentedly.

3

We set out for the station before dawn and queued up to buy tickets. And the train followed the shore of the Java Sea. Sometimes our train raced cars and we watched the sight with annoyance. Dust which was raised by the cars—dust which was mixed with various kinds of horse and human dung, snot, spit—rose in clouds and settled on our skin. Sometimes we came across small children shouting at us, at the same time stretching out their caps—begging. And this kind of thing had been going on since the railway line first opened and the train had sped out along its rails. When people threw their leftover food to them, they scrambled for it. But what I'm saying isn't really important.

The train went on and on. When it got to Rembang it began to veer south and pass through the teak forests and the ricefields. The closer we came to the town of my birth the clearer I pictured the narrow roads, the poor inhabitants, and father. Sometimes deer came into view running hard, frightened by the rumble of the train. And they ran into the scrub with their front legs and their back legs almost crossed, and their bellies doubled under them so that you could see the hunch on top.

The conductor who punched the tickets was still the same conductor as when I was a boy and often went to Rembang to see the seashore when the holidays came. But the conductor was already old and didn't recognize me. He didn't notice the people in the train. The only thing he noticed was the tickets.

I looked at my wife and said:

"Look how beautiful the forest is."

Without saying anything my wife bent her head to look out

of the window. Then she drew her head back in again and rested it against a corner of the train seat.

I looked at the beauty of the forest. I, too, had once gone into it—once when I was still a boy-scout and made a pilgrimage to the grave of Raden Adjeng Kartini.[1] The grave was not far from our train right now. Suddenly a ravine burst into view below my eyes. And spontaneously I cried:

"Look at that ravine. How deep it is!"

I looked at my wife. She opened her eyelids. And then the eyelids dropped and closed again.

I sighed.

I wanted to introduce her to the beauty of my home region with its ravines and its forests, with its deer and its monkeys. Yes, I wanted to very much.

Our train passed through stations and stopping places of which just the floors were left, lime-kilns, and piles of teak. And all of it brought back to me memories of my childhood when I had often gone sight-seeing on my bicycle in and out of the forest. Yes, it was a beautiful time, my spent childhood. And now I hymned its beauty in my memories.

When the train came within the city limits of Blora, I saw the square—and in the old days the buildings which had stood on the square. All at once I thought: it is the war which has destroyed those buildings. And a curiosity drove me to keep on looking out. Then suddenly I said:

"Let's hope the telegram got there anyway. And let's hope there's somebody at the station to meet us."

My wife opened her eyes. And as we looked at each other I said:

"We've arrived in Blora."

She packed things up. And I packed things up. Then the train stopped in the station of Blora. Again I poked my head out. But my eyes didn't light on anyone who I hoped might have come to meet us. And indeed the telegram, of course, hadn't arrived.

We carried our belongings. And the pony-trap which brought us to the house which I had abandoned all this time went along as calmly as it used to before. And the old cabman urged on his horse continually with his whip and with words—simply out of habit. There were many ruined buildings along the road. Of the P.T.T.[2] building which had been the pride of the people of the little town of Blora, there remained only concrete columns heaped up like pillows and bolsters. I took a deep breath. The pillar which commemorated forty years of Wilhelmina's rule was still standing. But its former beauty had gone. And the pillar was now painted pink. And I didn't understand why. Perhaps it was the "red" troops who had painted it when they had occupied our town.

And when our pony-trap stopped in front of the house which I'd left so long ago, my young brothers and sisters called out happily:

"Mas has come. Mas has come."

But they didn't want to come close, rather they kept their distance—those that were not yet grown up. Perhaps it was that they were shy because I now had a wife, a wife who was at that moment standing beside me. I didn't really know. Only those brothers and sisters who were already grown up came and helped me to carry out belongings.

When I entered the house, my head bumped against the roof beam. And then it struck me, I've become tall now. When I left this house, that roof beam was still high above my head.

4

We sat in the room at the front. My little brothers and sisters who were not yet adult and who appeared to be hesitant and like young pets, now began to come closer. And we chatted a lot about Djakarta, about Semarang, and about cars. Chatting is one kind of work that isn't boring but pleasant, and usually goes on and on. And then I asked:

"How's father's health?"

And my second sister, the third after me, replied slowly and carefully.

"We got the pills and blankets you sent for father. And I also got your postal order, and I used it to buy milk and eggs as you asked."

My wife and I listened in silence. She went on.

"I also got the shirt for father from the post office. The blankets, the shirt and the pills I've already taken to the hospital. But father said, *just take them all home*. So I brought them back."

I was startled and asked:

"And the pills?"

"He has already gone through one tube."

I felt a bit happier.

"And the milk and eggs?" I asked again.

"Father doesn't like them. *I'm fed up with eggs and milk*, father said."

I couldn't say anything. I looked at my wife. But from the expression on her face I got no reply. I cast a glance outside the house. I could see the orange tree which father had planted long ago. The tree had withered and was almost dead now.

"And father's health?" I repeated the question. My sister, the same one, didn't reply. Her eyes became red and moist.

"Why don't you answer?" I said, afraid.

"Yesterday and the day before, father just smiled—he smiled a lot. But just now, just now . . ."

She was silent. I didn't force her to carry on with what she was saying. I was silent too. For quite some time we bowed our heads. Even the youngest child who had begun to dare to ask questions didn't say a word. It was only half past twelve. And the sound of frying in the kitchen could be heard plainly. And then my sister continued in a voice that was still slow, obscure and careful:

". . . and this morning . . . father didn't smile any more. His voice had become so low it was almost inaudible."

She didn't go on.

"And what did the doctor say?" I asked.

"The doctor never says anything to us. There's only the one doctor here. And there isn't even enough medicine."

And then my first brother, who, as it happened, had got leave from his commanding officer, said:

"I've already asked the doctor about father's health. He said, I know what your father's illness is."

"Is that all he said?" I asked.

"Yes that is all—then I was asked to leave."

Again an atmosphere of earnestness was felt. Each person was lost in his own feelings and thoughts. Without my realizing it my second sister turned the conversation in a new direction. She said that my sister, the one just above her, who was already married, was in Blora at the moment. And quickly I asked:

"Where is she now?"

Her hand pointed to the door of a room. And everyone's eyes followed the direction in which she was pointing. And in my mind I pictured the face of my sister—and in the picture she was thin. I knew she was not well. But my lips said:

"Ask her to come out."

My sister went and opened the door of the room gently. Everyone's eyes were on her. She disappeared into the room. Then she came back out with her eyes red. Half-crying she said:

"*Mbak*'s[1] still sleeping."

And we chatted about other things. But soon my sister, the

one who was ill, was imagined again in my mind. It was simply on her account that I had sent the letter to father—that letter which was harsh because he didn't do anything about her illness. But at that time I was still in prison. And father had replied:

Yes, my son, throughout my fifty-six years of life I've known that men's efforts and choices are very limited. I wouldn't have let your sister go sick if I had any control over man's fate. She contracted the illness when she, too, was surrounded by red troops in the marsh area, the malaria area. And perhaps you yourself can understand what the situation was with medicines in the war zone—especially if one wasn't a soldier.

This reply melted my anger. And I heard in my breast the question "Was I wrong to send that harsh letter?" And the reply came by itself, "Yes, you were wrong." And because of that reply I felt guilty up till now—for I still hadn't met father again. But the continual flow of conversation took away all unpleasant memories. I saw the six brothers and sisters who were gathering around us—me and my wife—beginning to feel free of the atmosphere of earnestness. But I was still preoccupied with oppressive thoughts and memories.

For an hour we talked. I knew this from my watch. And then I looked at the smallest child and said slowly:

"Go, look at your elder sister, maybe she's already woken up."

He got up. And went right up to just in front of the door and called out in his child's voice:

"Mbak, mbak, mas has come."

He disappeared into the room.

No one watched him. The conversation picked up again. And then the young child came out of the room and the talking died. The child approached me. He whispered, "Mbak's crying."

I took a deep breath.

Slowly I got up. Went to the room. And stretched out on the iron bedstead without a mosquito-net, with only half a piece of *kain*[2] for a blanket, was my sister. She had covered her eyes with her arm. And I lifted her arm away. I saw a pair of eyes looking at me. And the eyes were red and filled with tears. I hugged her. She cried and I cried too. And through my tears I heard my own voice saying:

"Why are you so thin?"

She brought her crying more under control, so that it wouldn't become a torrent. And then I did the same.

"I've been ill a long time, mas," I heard her broken voice say.

"Have you been to the doctor?" I asked—in a broken voice as well.

"I've been to the doctor, but it's still just the same," came her broken voice.

"Perhaps it would be better if you went to a big town. There are many specialists there," in my broken voice.

There were only sobs.

"Have you had any children, *'dik*?"[3]

"Yes, mas."

"Where are they?"

My crying was already calmer. But my sister's sobs increased now. She replied in an empty voice:

"He's no more, mas. He's no more . . ."

She withdrew the arm which I was holding and again she covered her eyes. I took out my handkerchief and I wiped away her streaming tears.

"What do you mean by no more?" I asked.

"My child was born when it was only six months. It cried once. I was there to hear it cry. Then God asked for him back."

Once more I cried. Once more she cried. I heard nothing now except the storm which beat in my chest. And what I saw was only an emaciated body, a piece of blanket cloth, a mattress which only half-covered the bedstead, and ironwork together with crisscrosses of bamboo beside the mattress sticking out.

"You're still young, love, and you've still the hope of having other children," I said to cheer her. "Where's your husband?"

"Training in Semarang, mas."

The crying of us both in that room eased. Finally it died.

I arranged her blanket. I kissed my sister on the cheek and said: "Go to sleep."

She withdrew her arm from her eyes. She was calm now. Slowly she closed her eyelids. Once more I kissed her cheek which had once been full but which was now withered. Then I left the room.

5

The only transportation that most people in our small town can use is the pony-trap. The hospital lay two kilometers from our house. So on that afternoon we took a pony-trap to the hospital. Four of us went—I, my wife, my second sister and a young brother.

The hospital looked quiet. And patients from the charity ward sat outside on the verandah looking for lice in their hair, chatting, or dozing in their ward.

Room number thirteen—my father's room.

We entered slowly. The creaking of the door made father's eyes turn towards us. I saw father smile—the smile of a man who's satisfied with the life he's had on earth.

My wife and I walked in front and approached the bed. Suddenly I saw the smile disappear. And father's eyes rested on my face. Then I heard his voice which was almost inaudible:

"You!"

I moved closer to the bed.

Now father's eyes were closed. And blue circles surrounded the eyelids. Then I saw the tears gathering in his hollow eyes. And the tears stayed at the corners of his eyes—they didn't flow. And I also saw father's lips moving. I knew: father was crying and the crying had no strength to it. I looked toward the window, in the direction of the mortuary. I drew long deep breaths, one after the other.

Quickly I took father's hand. And now I saw his body which had once been so robust and now looked as thin as a slat of wood. I saw father open his eyes. Carefully and painfully he raised his hand which was now bone and skin. He stroked my hair. I heard his voice which was low, indistinct, empty and without strength:

"When did you arrive?"

"At twelve o'clock this afternoon, father."

"That was quick. Did you come by plane?"

"By train, father."

Father didn't say any more. He closed his lusterless eyes. I stood up and released my grip on his hand. And I saw father regulate his breathing. And I also saw that the breathing didn't stop at his chest. The breath came and went from his stomach and his stomach was continuously rising and falling. At times when father was seized with emotion, his stomach was shaken by his breathing. And I saw also that father's hair, which five years ago was still black, had now become white. And the moustache, the hair on his cheeks, and his beard which were black-white-gray made father's hollow face appear dirty.

"And this is your daughter-in-law, father," I spoke again.

And again father opened his eyes. He saw the woman who for six months now had been my wife.

"Come here," said father weakly.

And my wife came closer, and made her sembah. At that moment I felt extraordinarily proud that she was willing to make the sembah to my father. And father stroked her hair. In a voice which was indistinct, empty, low and without strength, he gave her his blessing:

"Selamat, ja, selamat, selamat."[1]

Father closed his eyes again. Suddenly a storm of coughing seized him. And father turned his body to the wall. When father had some relief from the coughing I heard him say:

"Don't come too close."

And we moved back. The storm of coughing attacked again. And his body which looked as thin as a slat of wood was racked by it, and we all watched—watched with an uncontrollable wrenching of our hearts. That storm of coughing eased and finally died away. Father dabbed at his mouth which was wet with spittle and phlegm which irritated his skin. He reached for the spittoon which was on the chair. He spat into it. And when the spittoon was put back on the chair we saw that the recent spittle was red. Yes, dark-red-blood! But we were silent, as if there was a long mutual understanding between us. I heard my wife whisper. "Ask father how he is." Like a parrot I mouthed out:

"How are you now, father?"

"Just the same, son. But those pills of yours managed to get rid of the foul smell in my mouth."

I saw father smile, as if he was saying thank you for having sent the pills.

"What do you think about being moved to a sanatorium?" I asked.

And father closed his eyes again. I saw him shake his head—shake it weakly. His voice came from far away:

"Oh, that can't be done now, son."

We were silent. But we each knew what was going on in the other's mind.

"Do you want some eau-de-cologne, father?"

"It would be nice if there was some."

I asked my sister to go and buy some eau-de-cologne.

"Would you like some cod-liver oil, father?"

His eyes opened. He smiled. Then his teeth showed. And his gums were still as pink as before. His voice came from far away.

"If I drink cod-liver oil—it will turn out to be a purgative."

I wept now, wept because I understood what would never be expressed.

Now and again we could hear the footsteps of visitors who had come to visit their families clattering into the room. And father watched me crying. But a little later his eyes were dimmed again. I was losing my father, my heart said. And, although after meeting him I didn't feel guilty any more, but—that oil! I was going to lose my father. Through my tears I could see a glass of milk which was still full; a bunch of bananas which hadn't been touched; food heaped on a plate; and the spittoon a quarter filled with spittle and phlegm with blood in it. I was going to lose my father. I glanced back and saw with my eyes hazy with tears my father's eyes encircled with blue, and closed. Only then did I wipe my eyes.

Then, for a moment, it was very quiet.

Suddenly father's lips moved. I heard his voice coming from his throat, low, faraway, indistinct and without strength:

"They didn't hurt you badly in prison, did they, son?"

Father's eyes remained closed. And I said no. I could make out a smile on his face. And a ray of happiness was drawn across his countenance.

My wife approached the bed. She asked gently: "Would you like to eat something, father?"

Father opened his eyes and turned his head to look at the white table—a hospital table—and at the plate which was still heaped with rice. We heard:

"Ah," but he was smiling. "Who's got the heart to eat meat the size of that."

And we looked at the meat piled on top of the rice—as big as the tip of a little finger. I bowed my head. Father's smile went away.

"What would you like to eat?" my wife asked again.

"Oh . . . ," his smile flashed again, "I don't want to eat anything."

His eyes closed slowly. His expression was tranquil.

When my sister came back bringing the eau-de-cologne, my wife quickly dabbed one of father's hands with it, and she laid that hand on his chest.

Father opened his eyes again, and he said gratefully,

"How refreshing."

He turned his body to face us and his right hand groped under his pillow. Then he brought out a pocket watch from underneath.

"It's half-past five. How quickly the day has gone."

I looked at my wristwatch and the hands showed half-past six. Outside it was beginning to grow dark. And my sister who had come with us whispered:

"If father looks at his watch that means we're being asked to leave."

I looked at my sister's face. But she was whispering in earnest. And father watched us all from his bed.

"Father, it's late." I said, "Excuse us if we go now."

Father smiled and nodded his head.

"Father—excuse us," said my wife.

"Father, excuse us," said my sister.

Father smiled again.

But my youngest brother went out of the door before us. We bowed slightly out of respect and left that room number thirteen. Outside I called the child:

"You must ask father to be excused."

He went back into the hospital room. And when he came out again I saw that he was crying—it was a crying which he tried to check. His eyes were red.

"Why are you crying?" I asked.

But he didn't answer. For a long time we waited for a pony-trap to pass. And while we were waiting in front of the hospital, my brother kept on crying.

"Why is he crying?" I asked my sister.

"He always cries when he comes home from the hospital."

And I didn't ask any further.

6

That evening my brother was still crying—three hours later. When we had all gathered in the front room talking together he had stayed by himself in the back room. Several times I called him but he wouldn't come. He was crying himself out. Four times I asked his elder sister to bring him into the front room, but he refused to come.

From the front room I saw him open his school books still crying. He read crying. He wrote crying. Slowly I got up from where I was sitting and approached him. He was studying Geography—but he was still crying too. And also crying, he learned by heart the names of places in Asia.

"Why do you keep on crying?"

At once, he shut his books. But reply?—no! He didn't want to talk. He kept on crying. I hugged him and I kissed his wet cheek. I know, my brother, I know: you're crying for father who's sick. And I came out with:

"Have you eaten?"

He only shook his head and wiped his tears on my lap.

"You'll come and sleep with me, won't you?"

"No."

"Let's go and sit out in front with the others."

"No."

I let him down from my lap and he ran away still crying. He disappeared into his room. And he didn't appear again. From where I sat all I could hear were his sobs rising and falling as if they were trying to call something which couldn't be called by a human voice. Slowly I went back into the front room and continued talking about Djakarta, about

Semarang, about cars, and about the many car thieves in Djakarta.

Then there came my uncle with his wife. And because it was the custom in our kampung that children couldn't join in the grown-ups' conversation, they left the front room and went to the back to study.

And as usual on the occasion of a meeting which marks the end of a long separation I heard:

"How are things?"

And I replied fine. And my wife was introduced to my uncle and his wife. The talking resumed. We each questioned and were questioned in turn. Coffee filled in the gaps. Then we became chatty. We came to:

"It looks as if your father is beyond help."

I watched my uncle's lips and his voice went on:

"Perhaps it would be a good idea to get some help from a *dukun.*"[1]

I looked carefully at his eyes. And his eyes looked at me in earnest. I also heard:

"I myself have only been to the hospital twice. Not because I don't want to go. I haven't the heart. That body which used to be so strong is now just bones. That ringing voice which used to slice through any opponent at every meeting now doesn't have any more strength. Those eyes which always made others bow their heads don't shine anymore. No . . . no . . . I don't have the heart to see them."

I bowed my head. It was as if his voice emphasized one thought: your father must die. I sipped my coffee and coughed a little.

"I don't know. I don't understand." I cried out weakly.

"Yes, I, too, don't understand. I don't know. I'm confused, too."

Before my eyes arose the black night—really black.

"Have you already been to the hospital?"

"Just this afternoon."

"How was your father?"

"I don't understand. I don't know." Again I cried weakly—so weakly my voice was almost inaudible.

"Perhaps your father has missed you for too long. How would it be if you stayed with him in the hospital? And if you wanted to write, you could write there."

I scratched my head in bewilderment. I said very slowly:

"To tell you the truth, I can't bear to look at father as he is now. I can't bear it. I haven't the heart."

We were all five of us silent.

"How's he eating?" my uncle suddenly asked. And my second brother replied sadly,

"Worse than yesterday or the day before."

"Let's hope that your coming brings him some relief."

"Let's hope so," we prayed.

But his voice was without conviction. And I felt that he didn't believe what he was saying himself. We were silent again. And everyone's thoughts pictured father's body slack and motionless on the hospital bed like a slat of wood. And we could hear, too, the coughing coming from right inside, weak, with hardly any force, a hollow, hacking cough. And I heard, too, "Oh . . . I don't want to eat anything."

"Tomorrow we'll look for a dukun." My uncle looked at me.

And I nodded. Together we sipped our coffee which was still warm. Our talk became chat. And our conversation again turned to Djakarta, Semarang, and car thieves.

Suddenly came:

"Where are you working now?"

"Balai Pustaka[2]—but I'd only been there three days when I left to come here."

"What did your boss say?" he asked.

"What did my boss say? He has no rights over what I say or over me personally."

The conversation died again. We went back to sipping coffee.

"It's not that which worries me so much," I said, "but the consequences of this." I continued rather more slowly.

"Yes," said my uncle.

And I didn't know whether he'd said this *yes* consciously or not. I saw him looking at my coffee cup vacantly. He, too, was confused. I heard him take a deep breath and he looked across at me. He said:

"And what are your plans now?"

"I don't know. I don't understand. I'm too confused."

I glanced at my wife. She was contemplating the darkness through the open door. I looked at my aunt. She was looking at a photograph on the wall by the light of the kerosene lamp on the table.

I sighed. And the night deepened.

7

I got up at nine in the morning. It was only after I'd washed that I got an opportunity to look around the house and the yard. In fact taking a wash wasn't a real wash. The water in our small town was thick with mud. We couldn't hope for piped water from a reservoir here. Perhaps it was this muddy washing water which made the inhabitants of our little town different from the inhabitants of big towns where the water was piped regularly from a reservoir, clear and good. Here people walked around with their skin cracked and split.

The house which I'd lived in when I was small was now visibly slanting. Some of the wall had already given way through age. The earth in our district is earth mixed with lime and clay. In the dry season, the clay earth cracks and tears up the stone floors.

In the garden, near the fence, I met our neighbor who was the same as before—he was a goat butcher.

"You've come, have you, *gus*[1]?" he asked with respect. "Aduh, you've been away so long, and now when you've come back, your father's sick."

I smiled at his interest. I replied:

"Yes, the war separated us for such a long time."

"You're grown up now. You've a wife, too."

I smiled again at his interest. Next I heard:

"There was a story that you were in prison."

I smiled again.

"Your father told us. You were beloved by the Dutch, he said. You had to stay with them. How many months were you in prison, gus?"

And I answered his question. And then I followed up my reply with:

"Blora's just the same as when I left it. Many new houses have been built and the old ones are now slanting." I looked in the direction of our house. I went on, "Our house, too, is tumbled down."

"Yes, gus. It was I who built that house long ago. At that time you were only just able to crawl. Twenty-five years ago. And all this time your house has never been repaired. Just think. Twenty-five years. That's no short time if you think about the poor quality of the earth here. Just look at those walled houses which were built after yours—all of them are already in ruins, falling to bits and split through. But your house is still strong." And now his voice became the voice of an old man giving advice. "If you can, gus, if you can, please try to repair your house. You've been away too long, and for too long you haven't mixed with the people here. Therefore maybe it's good if I repeat to you the old saying: If a house is falling apart, the people who live in it are falling apart, too."

He was silent. He wiped his old mouth. Then he bent his head. His eyes were looking at the big toe of his foot which he was idly moving. Then he went on in an apologetic tone:

"Your father's been in hospital forty days." And then his words came even more slowly. "A little while ago your father had just come out of hospital. And his health was good. His character seemed very much changed. Before, he never cared about anything except his work and a game of cards, lately he was always at home. Then suddenly we heard the news that he was sick again and had been taken to hospital."

I didn't comment on what he said. But he went on. Now in the tones of one giving advice:

"I hope your father will recover quickly thanks to your coming. And again . . . and again . . . what the old folks used to say, you still remember don't you? You still remember what I said to you just now? If a house is falling apart . . ."

"Yes," I took up.

"You're the eldest child, gus. I hope—even though I'm not

one of your kin or your close family—that you'll look after your house."

I nodded—but it was a heavy nod, made heavy by calculations as to the cost of wood, cement, nails. And I saw that the old man, too, understood the heaviness of the nod. But he didn't say anymore. And I, too, didn't say anymore. We had come to the end of what we wanted to say. This was a good opportunity to withdraw.

I looked at the well, too. It was twenty-five years old also. The bricks had already begun to crumble in places where people had been too rough in dipping for water. And the floor which surrounded the well had disappeared, sunk into the earth. In our poor area it's seldom that people dare to make wells. And in our dry area, a well is one of men's central concerns in life, besides rice and salt. And so, even if the well has been made at one's own expense, it eventually becomes common property. People who make wells are people who've contributed to the common cause in our area. And when a person owns a well in our area, he is respected by the inhabitants: more or less. And if you own a well here, and you shut up the well for your own personal use then you'll be shunned by people and they'll say you're mean.

The house and the well filled my thoughts now. The house was falling apart and its people, too, were falling apart. And that afternoon when I left for the hospital and met the goat butcher, without thinking about it further I came out with:

"*Pak*,[2] I'm going to repair the house."

He beamed as if the house was one of the important things in his life.

And on the way to the hospital I thought, perhaps father will approve of my idea too. The nearer I got to the hospital the surer I was in my heart: this time I'm bringing him medicine. And the medicine I gave to my father's ears to swallow was:

"Father, I'm going to repair the house."

But father was far weaker than he had been the day before. Very slowly he opened his eyelids and then he said with suffering:

"Yes, son, the house . . . the house . . . the house is too—too old."

It was as though he was saying something about himself.

I shut my eyes tight. He hadn't taken the medicine. For a long time I didn't ask him anything. And when I spoke again my words were:

"Father, what are you really thinking?"

I saw father draw breath. And I saw him search for strength in the breath which he had just drawn. His dry lips smiled. Then his eyes encircled with blue opened a little. He laughed. Some of the laugh I could hear, just a little of it. Then he went on in a voice of surrender:

"There isn't . . . anything . . . I'm thinking about, son," he said very weakly.

I cried.

Father closed his eyes again.

For a long time there wasn't any sound, neither from father, nor from me. Then, without any warning, I heard his voice weak, low, and fleeting:

"The w . . . well . . . repair . . . the wall around it."

"Yes, father." I replied.

For a long time there was no sound. Then I heard him go on:

"P . . . p . . . people need . . . water," he paused rather long and then went on, "in their l . . . lives."

He opened his eyes again. He looked at me. His mouth smiled: he thrust at me a meaning which wasn't expressed in words. Quickly, forcing myself to smile, I replied:

"Yes, father."

And his eyes closed again, just for a moment. Suddenly his whole body was racked. His eyes were open but they didn't look at anything. Then a storm of coughing seized him. And when he was like that, there wasn't anybody in the whole world who could ease his suffering. And I could only look on with a feeling of pain spreading in my chest. His pale face became bluish with the coughing. And when the coughing had relaxed I heard him say quickly:

"There's all sorts in a man's life."

He turned his head and looked at me. He called me:

"Come here. Close," he said quickly. "You're just married, my son. With a g-girl from . . . from . . . Pasundan.[3] You must . . . must remember that people's outlook in this area, Central Java, is . . . is different from that of people . . . who were born in, in, in West Java. You understand?"

"I understand, father," I said carefully.

"So, son, watch what you say and what you do; I hope—I hope, yes, I hope you won't hurt, hurt, hurt her feelings."

Father was silent. He looked at me with a look which implied great hopes. Slowly his eyes closed. Quickly I said:

"Yes, father."

He cleared his throat a few times swallowing the globs of phlegm.

"It's already night," he added.

And I remembered what my sister had said: this was a sign I should go. I approached my father's bed and gently felt his dry feet. My heart was torn. Weren't these feet once like my feet and hadn't they wandered here and there? And now these feet were lying idly on a mattress of a hospital bed. It wasn't his wish. No. It wasn't his wish. It seems that men don't forever have free use of their bodies and their lives. And some day this would be true of my feet. I saw father open his eyes at my touch. And I also saw him smile—but it wasn't the smile of a person who was living—it was a strange smile, a smile which contained a warning. 'This life, son, this life doesn't have any value at all. Just wait till the moment comes and then you'll realize that God created man on this earth in vain.'

I bowed my head. I said softly:

"Excuse me, father."

Father took out his watch. He looked at it a moment then his glance was directed at me. He nodded. And with a heavy tread I went leaving that house of the sick—a house which was the abode of those who weren't free to use their own bodies and their own lives.

8

Perhaps because I've several times seen strange things in this world, and perhaps also, because I've four or five times practiced mysticism, or perhaps because I'm weak, or perhaps because of other reasons which I'm not aware of, I still somehow believe in the power of dukun. I don't clearly know why.

And after the beating of the big mosque drum at magrib we—I and my uncle—left to look for a dukun. In fact the words *look for* are not quite appropriate, but out of respect for dukuns, these words are always used in our area.

The man whom we called a dukun was a teacher in a state primary school outside the town. The custom in our area of beginning any important conversation with trivial chat still held. So it was that we talked about Djakarta, about Semarang and about car thieves. And the dukun chatted about oranges and cassava in his yard, about his pupils, and about the situation during the Dutch occupation.

Finally my uncle said:

"To tell the truth we came here because we need help."

And as usual, although he already knew quite well why we had come, our host asked us in all sincerity:

"What help do you need?"

My uncle continued with the customary forms of respect in our area.

"We've come to request a medicine to cure my brother's illness."

And the dukun asked to be excused for a little while and then he went to the back of the house. My uncle looked at me and asked:

"You often come here if there's a problem?"

But I didn't answer. Within me there was emerging a struggle—the struggle which usually emerges when one is confronted with the power of a dukun. Could a dukun really help a sick man whom the doctor himself had given up? But *hope* made the struggle vanish: that dukun had the power, he must have the power. And this hope made me believe in him.

Then the teacher-dukun came out. His expression was clear and innocent like a child's and his eyes sparkled. It was easy for me to guess the reason: he had just finished meditating.

My uncle and I looked at him silently but he still didn't say anything. Two or three times he shifted his position. Then we heard him say slowly and earnestly:

"Yes, my friends, each man has his own destiny and there is nobody who can change that destiny."

He was silent and looked at us in turn.

"What do you mean?" my uncle asked.

"I mean that when I meditated I didn't find anything."

He bowed his head.

We looked at him silently, our hearts thumping, wanting to know more.

"Perhaps," he went on, this time looking at me with a long stare, "it's because your father is more advanced than me in these matters. I admit this."

"So you can't give us any help?" I asked, in a panic.

"I can only give you a *sjarat*[1]."

He fumbled in his pocket and took out of it a piece of incense. He continued in a steady voice:

"This isn't a cure, it's only a sjarat. You may dissolve it in your father's drinking water. Let's hope, God willing, your father can recover. But I myself can't say anything."

The three of us bowed our heads as though we were afraid to look at one another. Then I saw my uncle take the incense and put it in his pocket. It was only slowly that our conversation revived. Then the dukun reminisced.

"To tell the truth I owe a debt of gratitude to your father," he said. "It was he who placed me here. And I myself live now outside the town. I was placed here when the Dutch were still around. And your father ordered me to reopen the school. I said: *I'm afraid to be a Dutch official outside town.* He only laughed when he heard my excuse. And I explained my fear. Then he said. *Trust me. Nothing's going to happen to you.* And I, too, rolled up my sleeves and worked.

"On the opening day three times as many pupils came as in the Dutch period. We were short-handed at the school. And three days after the opening my house was visited by our troops from the edge of town. They said: *If you continue with the opening of the school, we'll burn it down.* Then I replied, repeating what your father had once said. *Even in war time schools have to be open. As for the opening of this school, even though it's at the expense of the Dutch Government, it's we who are going to enjoy the benefits.* And the soldiers accepted the argument. The school wasn't burned down. Yes, right up to the present it is still standing. I came to realize later on that your father was in fact a leader of the guerrilla administration—even though he was a school inspector appointed by the Dutch."

He was silent. Then he laughed a little. Finally the conversation came round to schools and teachers. Respectfully he asked:

"How many years was your father a teacher?"

My uncle replied, pleased by the question,

"Thirty years."

"How strong he must be. I've only been in service eighteen years but I've already got the feeling that I'm not up to it any more. But who wants to be teachers apart from us here? Teachers stay teachers forever. But during that time their pupils become important people. But teachers stay teachers. During my years of service I once had a heart attack. And if your father now has tuberculosis after thirty years of service—that's a sign of strength. He's very strong."

He was silent and looked at the road. A truck rumbled by, going east, in the direction of Tjepu. From the Dutch occupation till now our district has often been traversed by motor vehicles, a lot more frequently than before the Japanese landing.

"Perhaps he caught the illness when he was a school inspector—each day pedaling his bicycle fifteen to twenty kilometers," my uncle said.

"No," said our host, "having been a teacher for all this time, I can say no. I assure you his illness wasn't on account of that. Because he asked to become a teacher again, that was the reason. Fifteen to twenty kilometers pedaling a bicycle is a small matter for a teacher. What's hard is teaching, swallowing the bitter taste of the miseducation which parents have given their children. That's the thing which so easily breaks a teacher. It's even worse in a secondary school such as he taught in. Working in a secondary school is relatively light work if classroom discipline is maintained. Just imagine if the pupils in the class are altogether out of control. Just imagine . . ."

He didn't continue. He sat in silence as if he was at that moment remembering a particular pupil who had once so distressed him. Then he continued with a voice of experience:

"Once," he said slowly, "I hit a pupil. The following day he asked for permission to be absent because his father had been recently appointed to be *bupati*[2] at Rembang. I was quite taken aback. It was the son of a *patih*[3] I'd hit. And who was I? I was only the son of a common farmer. I was terrified. The boy's father was bound to come and thrash me because I'd dared to strike his son. And a week later . . ."

He looked at us. I heard him gasp as if it was still that time when he was afraid, afraid and waiting for the arrival of his letter of dismissal.

". . . the bupati from Rembang came in his car. When the car entered the school yard, there was already a feeling inside me: Now comes the quittance. Tomorrow I probably won't be able to come and teach again. And I'll probably live without the possibility of expecting a salary any more. And when the bupati put his feet on the threshold of the school, he immediately asked for me. And I faced him with a beating heart. But . . ."

He sighed deeply—a sigh of relief, and went on:

". . . he hadn't come to thrash me. No. On the contrary. He thanked me because I'd taught his son a lesson. He himself had reached the point where he couldn't educate his own son, he said."

I saw him smile with relief. And his moustache, like an umbrella over his mouth, took part in the smile of relief. He went on:

"And then I experienced a tremendous sense of joy—the most tremendous in my life."

We laughed a little. Our host sucked at his moustache. Eventually he carried on with his story:

"Because of that, when I asked the students who were about to leave school, *Which of you is going to go on to teacher training school?* Out of fifty pupils only three raised their hands. Apart from them, everyone else wanted to go on to ordinary secondary school. How sad I felt then. And I said to them, *If out of fifty people only three want to become teachers who is going to teach your children later? And suppose you go on to become a general, will you be satisfied if your children are taught by the son of a saté-seller?* None of them replied. Then I gave some advice to those who were going to become teachers. *If you're not absolutely sure, abandon your ideals of becoming a teacher,* I said. *A teacher is a victim, a victim forever. And his duty is far too heavy—opening the source of goodness which lies hidden in the bodies of the country's children.* And the three children said in earnest, *We want to become teachers however hard it may be.* And I nodded my head to the three of them."

Then I felt that family background was still absolute in the district of Blora and that a teacher's lot—even if he is looked upon as a father by the people—is full of disappointments. But I didn't ask any more questions. I could see it all in my own family.

As we bicycled home my uncle said:

"Because I am a teacher myself, I can tell you that your father's influence among the teachers here is very great and much felt."

I didn't reply.

"If your father was allowed to receive visitors besides his family, they would all come to look in at the hospital. It's lucky that it's not allowed. If it was, well I'd feel sorry for your father.

I didn't agree or disagree. My uncle continued:

"If a dukun during his meditation can't come up with anything, that's a sign that . . . but let's hope he'll be all right."

9

That afternoon I visited the hospital with my wife and my two sisters. My wife fed father some broth spoon by spoon. And it was then that I felt how easy it was for someone to be close to another through common humanity. I was moved. Truly I was moved by this small insignificant action. Taking it with pauses my father's throat swallowed the soup. And each swallow was accompanied by a clicking sound. Yes, it was as if the sound didn't come from his throat. Twelve spoonfuls! How pleased I was. Usually, father didn't eat as much as that. And there came the voice of hope: "Perhaps father's beginning to get better now."

I saw father close his eyes again. And his weak voice followed: "Enough. That's enough."

My wife put the soup on the table and we sat down on the empty bed opposite father's. Father had become so thin. He was thinner than when we first came. And I remembered our conversation of the night before.

"We must go home soon," said my wife. "If not, our funds don't permit us . . ."

And I agreed with what she said. And when father opened his eyes, I quickly approached his bedside. Slowly I said:

"Father, what do you think, supposing we go back to Djakarta?"

Father was silent. I looked at his eyes, circled with blue. And I saw tears gather in the corner of his eyes. I moved back a little, further away. And I saw, too, father's stomach heaving convulsively. I was taken aback and immediately regretted having spoken that sentence. And when the convulsions had eased, father wiped his eyes and looked at my wife. I noticed the forced smile sketched on his lips. And then in a strained voice:

"Wait a little while, all right? Stay another week."

And my wife returned his smile and father, too, was still smiling. And then that smile disappeared and his eyes closed. The blue circles seemed to have got bluer. Then I saw his eyes grow moist again and his stomach begin to heave. I saw my sisters crying when they saw that. And I cried too. Why was I crying? I didn't know. And why did father ask for one more week? I didn't know. But father had asked for a week. And I was crying. Again there came to me that feeling: Father's going to leave us. Father's leaving us. And my tears streamed down more and more. I saw father cover his face with his white handkerchief. His stomach convulsed even more. When he took away his hand from his face his eyes weren't moist any more but they were still closed. His breathing became regular again. We heard him say slowly:

"It's already dark, my children!"

But his eyes were still firmly closed. It was only when we began to excuse ourselves that those eyes were opened again. We left. I stayed behind a little. And when the younger ones had already gone out of the door, I went back in. I peeped at father from behind the white muslin curtain. And I saw him sobbing like a man who's afraid of losing something. All at once, I broke into a flood of tears which I'd kept pent up in my chest.

"Father! Father!" I cried in my heart.

Then I, too, ran out of the room wiping my eyes.

Again came the feeling of regret at having uttered that sentence. And from that day on there was a considerable change in father's health. In the week that followed he made lots of requests. *Lele*[1] fish! And my wife and my sisters cooked some lele fish. But father wouldn't even taste it. Then father's craving changed again. Papaya! And a sherbet of papaya was also made. But father only drank two spoonfuls. And there were many other requests. But those requests remained just requests. His health grew worse. The last thing he requested was ice. Ice!

And again ice. Although ice had been forbidden by the doctor, we ignored this to please father.

"Son, ice," he said when we entered his room. And after the ice had slid down his throat, he beamed. He said:

"My breathing, son, my breathing comes . . . comes easier . . . if . . . if . . . if I take ice."

And with a feeling of anxiety we watched father sometimes eating whole slivers of ice.

One evening in the pitch black courtyard my uncle said:

"Your father does nothing but look at the time. And he asks for a lot now, and what he asks for is only because it's a passing whim. Both are signs that . . ."

He didn't go on.

He took his bicycle which he had leaned against the post of a fence. Then he got on it. He looked back and said:

"I'm going home. It's already late."

And he disappeared into the blackness of the night.

What he said had a great effect on me. That night I deliberately didn't go to sleep. My sister, the third child after me, stayed up as well.

The two of us sat opposite each other facing the oil-lamp. We talked about a lot that night. And I asked:

"What was it like during the 'red' occupation?"

She didn't reply to my question immediately. She thought a little. Only then did she reply:

"I can't say much. Father was arrested by the 'red' troops."

"Yes I've heard that. But why was he arrested?"

"I don't know, mas."

"And how did you live all the time father was in prison?"

She did not reply. I saw her eyes fill with tears. And a communication which was clearer than a reply was reflected in those eyes filled with tears. I didn't press her.

"How did father get free from the 'reds'?"

"Father was imprisoned in the jail here, then he was marched to Rembang. And when they got to Rembang the Siliwangi division had already begun to enter the district and father was freed. But mother's brother-in-law was killed here."

"Yes. War's really a curse for man," I said, comforting her.

"War forces man to examine himself. Because, little sister, in one's self there lies everything there is in the world and everyone else feels this is so, too."

I faltered. My words were really intended for myself and were not meant for my sister at all. And my sister said: "Yes."

We were silent for a while. The wind blew gustily outside. And when the wind died down, we could hear the talking of the watchmen in their shelter. My sister continued:

"When father came back, he was so thin."

"And when the Dutch invaded?"

"The Dutch didn't enter Blora right away, mas. They were held up for several hours in Mantingan—five kilometers from here. But our troops didn't have any heavy arms. So the Dutch eventually entered. But that short battle was enough to warn us to assemble our forces on the other side of the river."

She was silent. She looked at me. Then she pointed towards the south. She went on.

"And father also escaped to the other side of the river."

"And how did you and the family manage to live during that time?"

When she heard my question she hesitated. Slowly she replied:

"At first we sold whatever we could. We went into petty trading. People were happy to buy from us. Then they gradually began to buy on credit because money was hard to get. And then . . . then they didn't want to pay their debts. It's true, mas, it was as though they were happy to see us go under."

She was silent again and I saw the tears in her eyes. And they didn't stay in her eyes. They began to trickle and she sobbed. Then she finally burst into tears.

"Oh . . . they . . . as though they didn't know that father was at that moment fighting for the Republic."

"Let it rest, adik, let it rest. What's done is done. Don't grieve over it. You still have a brother. And I'm going to work as hard as I can for the welfare of all of you."

She wiped away her tears hurriedly.

"The world really is a strange place, little sister," I spoke again. "If one family succeeds in getting ahead, people become envious and angry. They always find something at hand to abuse and insult people behind their backs. But if a family is ruined, people gather to jeer them on and help to ruin them. I know, little sister, that's the way things are in small towns. Because the people in a small town don't care about anyone but themselves, their family and their surroundings. It's different in a big town. There's a lot that people care about there. So, little sister, it's better not to interfere in their business. You understand, don't you?"

And once more I faltered. This advice I seemed to be giving myself and not her. My sister nodded, and said:

"Yes, I think so, too."

"Yes. We can't expect anything from them. If we have to expect at all, we have to expect from ourselves."

"Yes, mas."

"In the old days we were always happy because, because at that time we were still small. And now, we really feel how bitter this life is, when we constantly remember the malice of others. But for us, isn't it true that we don't need to do wrong by others?"

"It's true, mas. I don't want to do wrong by others."

"That's enough, little sister, more than enough."

We were silent again. Then in a low voice I gave her some advice and, as before, this advice, too, was really intended for myself.

"We'll build a new family, with our own resources and for ourselves. It's all right if we become an island on its own in the middle of the ocean. If we fall, we fall without a cry. If our island sinks into the ocean, then we sink by ourselves and there's no one to see us. I too, little sister, I too, am fed up with all this. I'm fed up with all this empty politeness. Oh . . . I don't understand. I don't know anything any more."

My sister didn't reply. And I didn't go on with what I was saying. I gulped the coffee which she had put there for me. Then she spoke again:

"Eventually father was caught by the Dutch, too. Father came out of the forest and was heading for Ngawen. You haven't forgotten Ngawen have you?—five kilometers to the east of Blora."

"Why should I have forgotten? I used to go there a lot before."

"At the time father was sleeping in a small mosque. And when he opened his eyes he was already surrounded by Dutch troops aiming their rifles at him. That was father's story when he returned home. He brought back a bamboo basket. And in that basket he had kept a bottle for drinking water, one pair of underclothes and a *destar*.[2] Father came back using a walking stick. At the time I was really alarmed. Quite suddenly father had become old, mas."

She was silent again after uttering the word "old." Once again her eyes filled with tears. I didn't press her. And when the emotion had passed she continued:

"Quite suddenly there were more white than black hairs on his head. Father spoke much less than he used to. He was appointed by the Dutch to become a school inspector. His salary was big, mas. His allotments of food were extraordinarily large. But he was very seldom at home. You know father liked to gamble. But his expeditions during the occupation weren't just to gamble, mas, not at all. Father kept fighting for the life of the Republic. All the soldiers knew this, mas, all of them. And you perhaps don't know yet what happened after father had worked for the Dutch."

She was silent again and gulped in the evening air in large draughts. I shook my head. She continued in a voice as though she were reciting a litany.

"It was like this, mas, every day letters arrived here from men at the front as well as from people who called themselves non [cooperators]. You know what those letters were, mas? Begging letters! They asked for help. And every day it was the same. And none of the letters did father allow to go unheeded. None of them. All of them had to be given attention. Sometimes, mas, yes, sometimes I didn't receive housekeeping money, not even a cent, even though it was to buy food for father himself—and that was for a whole month. And all this, mas, all this reminds me of the kindness of a Chinese friend. When father was still in the guerrilla area and during the time of the 'red' occupation as well, this Chinese friend helped us a lot. And I didn't understand why he was willing to keep our family from the danger of starving."

"Yes, little sister, common humanity sometimes joins together men from different poles. And in this case common humanity joined us with someone from the Heavenly Kingdom."

"Yes, mas," said my sister in an aimless voice. Then she carried on with her story. "Then father worked too much for the Republic. And when we got independence father fell ill. For three months he was treated in the hospital. But father still worked a lot. Finally he realized that his health didn't permit it, and one by one he surrendered his offices in the political and social movements. But his former health didn't return. He fell sick again, and that's how he's been ever since. The doctor says it's tuberculosis. And when I asked here and there whether father could possibly be put in a sanatorium, mas, my question remained just an echo. There wasn't a single voice that dared to reply. If there was a reply, the reply was only: *sanatoriums are very expensive nowadays.* And if that wasn't the reply it was, *sanatorium?* the sanatorium's full of businessmen. If you're a civil servant but not an important civil servant, don't even think that you can get a place in a sanatorium."

She was silent again and she stared at me a long time. I shook my head. And I didn't know what to think. My sister bowed her head and went on:

"And, mas, father himself was offered the chance to be a member of the local assembly. And he refused the appointment."

"Refused it? Wasn't that an ideal opportunity to improve the conditions of the people?" I asked.

"I don't know. Father only said this, he said, *local assembly*? The local assembly is only a stage. And I don't fancy becoming a clown—even a big clown. And father persisted in refusing the offer. He even got the opportunity of becoming the coordinator of education to organize the teaching in the whole Pati region. But he turned that down, too, and said, *My place isn't in the office. My place is in the school.* Yes, perhaps it was that attitude which made father not want to go on as a school inspector and to become a teacher again. And father also said, *we teachers in this country of ours, we must not reduce our numbers, even by one man.*"

"Yes," I said aimlessly.

She sipped her coffee. I smoked. The smoke rose. I saw her eyes suddenly resentful. She asked me circumspectly:

"Do you still remember Sami, mas?"

"Yes, I still remember her."

And in my mind I saw a small coquette of a girl who had become her family's bait—bait swallowed by the Japanese.

"She was absolutely delighted to see our ruin. And she used to say to the neighbors about father, *Of course he surrendered himself to the Dutch on purpose,* according to her. *A man who follows the Dutch really is a sheep.* He's not a man, she said, too. Sometimes she said that kind of thing to her friends when we were in the vicinity. Oh I couldn't bear it—I couldn't."

"Why did you pay any attention to the words of somebody who didn't have any idea how to behave?" I said emptily.

". . . I wasn't prepared to hear talk like that. And father who was sick, whose life in the world was spent only in being asked by people for help, who had already sacrificed his career and his health . . . only to become the subject of talk of people like that."

She was quiet again. And this time she remained silent a long time. And as for me I didn't want to break in on her thoughts. I felt in myself that she was looking for a channel to pour out her grievances.

Second by second slipped away, swallowed by the night. And, unnoticed, man's age slips away second by second, swallowed up by the night and the day. But men's problems are ever green like time. They show themselves everywhere, and they attack men's minds and hearts everywhere too, and sometimes they go away, and what they leave behind are minds and hearts, empty as the sky.

Sometimes we could hear the drum from the watchmen's shelter in front of our house beating. And this drumming was picked up by others from other shelters. And the silence of the night didn't check the outpouring of my sister's grievances. Carefully she continued:

"During the time when you were gone, mas, grandfather died. And then grandmother came to live with us. You were still in prison then. We knew about your imprisonment from your letter which you sent through the Red Cross. Grandmother stayed with us for several months. And one day, mas, one day a neighbor of hers who'd lived next to her old house—on the edge of town—died. She went to pay her last respects. She was gone a long time. Three days. And I didn't understand why she'd gone to pay her respects to her neighbor for as long as that. Then someone came here and told us, and told us, mas. Your grandmother has died there, two hours after catching a stomach complaint."

She was silent and looked at me. And I said:

"I heard about that, too, from the letter which your sister sent me."

"Yes . . . but you don't know how upside down we were then. Yes, mas, at that time father was in the guerrilla area. And what I don't understand is why she died there."

"She'd lived there more than thirty years and grandfather, too, had died there. Sometimes, sometimes people feel too close, too much in love with the plot of land where they've lived for so many years, a plot of land which for so long has given them a place to live, which has for so long provided them with its produce to eat. And sometimes people want to die in the bosom of that plot of land where they've lived. Yes and sometimes, little sister . . ."

She was silent and I saw her eyes filled with tears. She was remembering all the bad times which had passed like a procession in her life. And I continued:

"And sometimes . . . sometimes . . . their wish is granted and they do die in the bosom of the earth where they've lived so long."

"But, mas . . ." she interrupted.

"But?"

"It was me, only me who went to attend to things there because the younger ones were still too small and the older ones were in prison or out in the guerrilla area. Perhaps you're right; she wanted to die in the bosom of that plot of earth where she'd lived for more than thirty years. But mas . . . but," she faltered. But she looked at me. And when she saw I was looking at her, immediately she shifted her gaze to the door behind me. She went on in a scared voice:

". . . but her mouth, puckered up tight . . . yes I saw it when she was being washed—it's that, it's that which I always see in my memory. And that mouth, that mouth, it's as if it wanted to express that she didn't like the treatment which had been given her as she faced her death."

She sighed.

I sighed.

There was silence.

And the night outside went on swallowing the span of men's lives. I shook my head which was picturing the sentences which my sister had just spoken. I said:

"I don't understand."

"Even I don't understand, mas . . . but that mouth of hers, that mouth, that mouth that seemed as if it wanted to say to me why is it that I'm only allowed to enjoy a fraction of happiness on this earth? Why? Perhaps all this occurred just because I was very affected by what happened. Perhaps, yes, perhaps. But that was the state of my feelings and thoughts. And I couldn't suppress them."

Suddenly she was quiet. And all of a sudden she broke into sobs. I got up from where I was sitting and I hugged her. I stroked her hair. I heard her say in a halting voice:

"Mas, mas, I, I wasn't ready to let grandmother die in someone else's house. I wasn't ready. I couldn't accept it. She didn't receive the care which people should have when they are leaving the world forever."

And I comforted her with empty words:

"Isn't it all in the past, little sister? And what's in the past can never be repeated."

"But I wasn't ready to let it happen, mas. I wasn't prepared to."

"You have to accept everything once it's happened," I said.

And then I, too, felt that I wouldn't have been ready to let grandmother receive insufficient care when she was dying. And I let my tears come, too, tears which had flowed continuously since the moment I had set foot again in Blora. I was at the end of words to say. And I was silent. My sister who knew that my tears, too, were flowing didn't say anything. And her crying became heavier.

And as those tears trickled away, so men's lives trickled away, scattered over the face of the earth, disappearing, never to be seen again. And every now and again we heard the flap of bats' wings as they roamed in the blackness of the night, in and out of the branches and leaves of the djambu tree. Yes, bats from tens of centuries ago—bats which lived safe in the night looking for their livelihood.

My sister gathered her sobs together in a long sigh.

"It's already three o'clock, little sister, perhaps it would be better if you went to sleep."

She shook her head and said:

"Tonight, like you, I will not go to sleep—for father's sake."

And quite suddenly father's body like a slat of wood was pictured again in my mind. And quite spontaneously I uttered words of regret:

"Supposing father had become a representative in the local assembly or had become coordinator, he would have been a high official. And perhaps if he had been a high official, a place would have been found for him in a sanatorium."

I was silent.

My sister was silent.

And the silence made me uneasy, so I forced myself to speak:

"But father wasn't willing to make use of an easy opportunity. He left that to others. Father . . ."

"Oh . . . father who always sacrificed himself for others. Father who was always sacrificed to others . . ."my sister burst out.

And then her outburst was spent and she cried again.

"We didn't look for all this, little sister," I said, comforting myself. "It all came without our asking. And we have to accept it. We just have to accept it. Men can do nothing in the face of something they don't understand."

"Why does there have to be war, mas?"

"Because we don't know, little sister. Because we don't understand."

"O . . . war, mas . . . war stole away our mother from us, and our youngest brother, our grandfather, our grandmother, and it also stole away father's health. Why, mas? Why should it happen like that?"

"Well . . . because we don't understand why, that's the reason."

"You're uncertain of yourself, mas, I've noticed you've been continually uncertain and at a loss these few days since you've been back in Blora."

"Yes, little sister, it's been like that. But you don't need to worry about me."

And I sipped the coffee which was already cold. I sat down in my chair again. Then I smoked a cigarette. The cocks were beginning to crow in their coops, followed by the sound of people, pounding grain [into flour]. The clock on the wall chimed five times. My other brothers and sisters were beginning to get up.

"It's five o'clock now, little sister. Let's go to bed. I'm going to sleep, too." And so we slept.

10

During that week nothing happened, except that father's health gave cause for increasing concern. When I looked in, father didn't want to eat as had been the case for the whole of that week. Ice! Ice that was always what he asked for. And because we didn't have the heart to disappoint him we always brought him ice. And when the factory in Rembang wasn't working because a machine was out of order, and we came to the hospital without any ice, we felt like guilty men who were being haled before a judge.

During that week, too, many people said to us:

"Why don't you just bring your father home?"

And the question kept gnawing at us. Should we bring him home? Should we? Having to reach a decision makes people uneasy. But when I reached the hospital I didn't say anything about what was gnawing at me. It was, on the contrary, father who said to me:

"Son, now you can go, go . . . return to Djakarta."

Hearing that I was startled. And I quickly said:

"No, father. We'll return later."

Father opened his eyes. He directed his smile at me, a smile which seemed to be testing me and said, "Haven't you stayed too long in Blora, and won't your staying too long interfere with your work there?" And I said further:

"I can postpone my duties in Djakarta, father."

Father shook his head. He shut his eyes again. And the circles round his eyelids appeared to have got bluer than yesterday and the day before. They were blackish now. He seemed to be very happy with my reply. And, after the atmosphere grew calmer, my brother said:

"How do you feel about coming back home, father?"

Father opened his eyes. He smiled. Then he closed his eyes again. He seemed to be thinking. Then we heard him say rather resolutely:

"Here, son, the nurses are all still like children." His eyes were open and he looked at the bell which was on the table. "If I ring the bell . . . if I want to go to the toilet, son, they don't come to help; just the reverse, they run still further away when they hear the summons of the bell. It's too much."

But he was smiling when he said those words.

"It's better if you stay at home," my brother said again.

"Ah! It would only mean a lot of work for people at home," he protested.

Then father began coughing. His thin hand gave us a sign to stand back. And we stood back.

When the coughing had died down, my sister gave him some spoonfuls of *tjendol hungkwe*[1] which had been chilled with ice. And we felt pleased because father was able to take fifteen spoonfuls. But father's health evidently couldn't be measured by whether he took a little or a lot.

11

It became very evident how father's wants and desires kept changing more and more frequently. That morning one of the male nurses who had been on night duty the evening before came to our house and presented us with a receipt—asking for an advance on his salary for the month of March. But it was now May. The receipt had been drawn up by father. I didn't understand why an advance for the month of March was being asked for. And when I asked my uncle he said:

"Since independence, teachers haven't yet been paid. It's almost half a year now."

And then I understood.

Three hours later I went to the hospital. Before I went in, I heard father groaning and complaining. His breathing was heavy and difficult and every now and again it was interrupted by a slight, low, painful coughing. Carefully I opened the door. On the bed I saw father sleeping limply. I approached on tiptoe. But father opened his eyes. He seemed to gather all his remaining strength. Then in a reproachful voice—a voice which reproached everything:

"Oh, oh, son—what was the point of keeping me waiting here on this bed?"

"I didn't understand the drift of what he was saying. And I was confused. Of their own accord my eyes dropped to the floor. And father went on:

"How many more days must I wait here?"

And I saw him screw up his eyes.

"What is it, father?" I asked confused.

"Oh! Oh!" He was silent a while in order to get rid of his coughing. He went on. "Didn't someone call at the house?"

"Yes, father."

His eyes opened again. Accidentally his glance fell on the pan full of soup which my sister had just put there. He added:

"What have you brought in that pan?"

My sister replied:

"Some broth, father."

"Oh! Oh!" His eyes shut again. "So the fellow didn't say anything to you?"

"He only handed over the receipt and asked for ten rupiahs."

"Oh! Oh!" father said again. And round his closed eyes there was a look of sadness, annoyance and pity for everything.

All at once a voice inside me said: the fellow this morning tricked you. But this voice was cut off just there. Father went on:

"I said, take me out of this hospital quickly."

I was taken aback.

"Didn't you read the note?"

"There wasn't a note, father."

"Oh . . . Allah."

Then father was silent again to recover his strength. And I saw his stomach heaving again. And then when the heaving of his stomach had died down I saw him gather himself together. He continued:

"Turn over the receipt. I wrote something on the other side."

And this time father really had exhausted himself. He didn't speak again after turning his body to face the wall. On tiptoe I stepped back and went behind the curtain with my sister and opened the receipt. And it was true. On the other side of the receipt there were some lines of scribbled writing, the letters unclear and showing the signs of having been rubbed by hands. It said:

"Son,
I can't stand staying in this hospital any longer. And since the family is all gathered it's better that I be taken home. Come to the hospital as quickly as possible.
Your father."

I looked at my sister. And she was looking at me. Then unconsciously our eyes dropped to the floor. I took a deep breath to steel myself. A little bit of courage entered. I went up to father and said:

"Father, right now I'm going to get permission from the doctor."

And father opened his eyes. He smiled, his usual smile. I went out immediately.

In our little town, there was only one doctor. In the Dutch period there had been three doctors. But it has always been true that death is to be found everywhere in time of war even when the war is a small one.

And now the doctor who was sovereign here sat like a king behind his desk. His voice had the tone of someone wanting to belittle everything he faced. He said:

"What do you want?"

"I'd like permission to take my father from room number thirteen."

He still remembered who was occupying room number thirteen. Immediately he replied:

"Granted, granted."

"And what about my father's health?"

The doctor shook his head, with a sovereign shake. My heart beat fast. In a panic I asked:

"Is there no hope?"

The shaking of his head stopped suddenly.

"Is there the slightest hope he'll recover?"

"There is," he whispered. "But it'll take a long time." He straightened his head and pierced me with a look. "You can take your father away. You can use the ambulance, and now you can go."

I heard the ring of a bell. And as I left the doctor's room, I heard him giving orders to one of his subordinates. Hurriedly I went to father's room. Happy myself, I passed on the happy news:

"Just a little longer, father."

Father's eyes remained closed. And I saw his lips smile. I waited for him to open his eyes, look at me, and speak again.

But he didn't say anymore. It was only when the attendants came bringing a stretcher that father opened his eyes and distributed his smile among them. And the attendants returned the smile—a smile which expected a return.

Along the way, in the Red Cross ambulance, father groaned continually. Sometimes he threw a glance out of the ambulance window to look at the green of the leaves. Father loved nature, plants, and animals. I'd known this since I was small.

A look of relief came to his face when he was back again, lying in the house where he had lived twenty-five years—the house where my brothers and sisters and I had grown up. And also the house where mother had closed her eyes for the last time. It was also the house which was falling apart. Falling apart! The words reminded me of what our neighbor, the goat-butcher had said: *if the house is falling apart . . .* And this recollection reminded me that I must repair it.

As it was customary in our area, the neighbors had to come when they heard that someone was seriously ill. They came only to chat together in front of the sick man, even though this wasn't their intention. And what else could they do except chat when they knew nothing at all about health and disease. And so one by one they came. And there was no good reason for my brothers and sisters and me to refuse entrance to those who had come, meaning well. Thus, as time passed, more and more people came to look in.

That evening father rested peacefully on his bed. Only the phlegm which interfered with his breathing felt as if it was stuck in my throat too. Now and again I looked in on him, at the same time spraying the area around his bed with DDT. And if, by chance, father happened to open his eyes, I was certain to hear his low voice, saying painfully and without force:

"You . . . don't need to stay up for me. Go to bed."

And I would answer:

"I'm not sleepy, father."

And then father would close his eyes again.

We took it in turns to stay up for father. And we felt deeply how happy one feels to stay awake for a father—one's own father—who is ill. And I felt how easy it is for men who live in suffering sometimes—on the quiet—to enjoy happiness.

12

If I'm not mistaken it had just turned eight that evening. My wife and I were walking together along a path about five hundred meters from the house. There was a lot I talked about with my wife. Mainly about the money situation.

"It would be better if we went back home, mas. You must think of our money situation," said my wife.

And as usual I replied to what she said with:

"I'm not going back to Djakarta before the situation here is quite settled."

And so we quarreled along the road. Money! Djakarta! Father! The house which was falling apart! And as usual the quarreling arose because we had different opinions and different reasons. The quarrel, which was conducted in whispers, wasn't resolved in any way. We only came to a point of deadlock when I replied:

"You can go back first. I'm definitely going to stay here until everything is settled."

And the quarrel stopped.

In silence we walked on, and we walked along a small town road which was quiet and with no asphalt surface. Many people were sitting on benches at the side of the road by the gutter enjoying the air of a small town on a cool peaceful evening when the sky is strewn with billions of stars. And we didn't talk any more. Each of us was worried by our own thoughts and our own inclinations. We entered the house again—the house which was dark because electricity hadn't reached our area yet. We heard father coughing—his low, painful, hollow cough without force. I went immediately to his room. By that time the coughing had ceased. I heard him say, testing me with a direct glance:

"What have you been quarreling about?" he asked.

I was startled.

And it showed: how father was concentrating the strength in his voice.

"What were you quarreling about?" he repeated.

I didn't understand what he meant and what he was getting at. I only looked at him. I wanted to ask him what he meant. But I didn't dare. And when his eyes, too, met mine I saw him smile. He carried on in a normal voice:

"Yes, yes, son! You don't need to quarrel any more. Really there's no need. Don't you know that on this earth it's just winning that's required? Winning, winning, winning . . ."

And he repeated those words in a voice which grew weaker as it went on, and finally became inaudible. Father dozed again. As usual when he dozed, the phlegm which blocked his breathing passage caused him to snore, which made me shudder. And I went and sat down on the couch opposite his bed.

And the night outside rolled on. The whole household was asleep. And I, too, fell asleep.

Whenever father coughed and awoke, one of us was sure to be there at his side. And usually we heard him whisper:

"Ice."

Sometimes the ice which we'd got had already melted because we didn't have a thermos in the house. Circumstances like that, it was difficult for us to bear. And if the ice was in fact quite gone we could only reply softly:

"The ice is finished, father."

And usually when father heard a reply like that, he immediately closed his eyes again. And if father coughed and awoke he would repeat again:

"Ice."

And if the sun had not yet risen the same reply would follow—a soft reply, difficult to utter:

"The ice is finished, father."

And father closed his eyes again until a new fit of coughing woke him.

That night, too, father was woken by his coughing, and that time it was I who came to him. He didn't ask about ice. But:

"What are you thinking about now, son?"

"I'm not thinking about anything, father."

"What have you written about the family?"

"I sent letters to Djakarta and to Kediri saying that you were seriously ill."

"There's something else which you haven't told me."

I was confused. I didn't understand what he meant. I asked:

"What do you mean, father?"

Quickly father closed his eyes. I heard him sigh. I felt more and more confused. Painfully his voice went on:

"T- try . . . try . . . asking."

Then he fell asleep again. And as he slept his continual groaning could be heard. It was this groaning which usually pursued us so that we were never able to sleep deeply and peacefully. And, as for his strange question, I didn't think about it again.

13

The incense powder which we'd been putting in father's drinks all this time didn't seem to have any effect on his health. This made us lazy about continuing with it.

That day it was very hot. In our region, an area which is surrounded by teak forests, it is scorchingly hot throughout the day and the cold at night and in the early morning is biting. And that particular afternoon—a day I'll never forget all my life—the heat was extraordinary. The wind blew gustily. The dust blowing here and there filled the scorching air. At the time I was tired after the previous night's exertion, and had dozed off. My sister came running to look for me. She said:

"Mas, father's talking about corn. I don't understand. He's also talking about corn being shot. I don't understand, mas."

I ran to father's room. And I found father being attended by my younger sister.

"Hold my hand, child!" he said.

I saw my sister take his hand. And father said:

"Ninety-nine grains of corn."

"Ninety-nine grains of corn." My sister repeated.

Father coughed and turned towards the wall—towards the east. Then I relieved my sister. And after father's fit of coughing had subsided he said to me,

"Hold my hand, son!"

I took his hand.

"Tight!"

I tightened my grip. And I felt his hot, trembling hand in mine. And with the forefinger of his right hand he pointed to the wall. He asked.

"Do you know what that is?"

"It's the wall, father."

Father groaned.

"No, no, not the wall. The east."

"Yes, father, the east."

"Over here, son . . ." he paused. He took a breath. He put all his strength in his words. He continued in a voice which was low, earnest, and calm. "Here, there were ninety-nine grains of corn put up as a prize. Understand?"

I became nervous, bewildered, and couldn't think. I replied. "I don't understand, father," I answered, frightened.

I heard father groan. After he had groaned I felt his grip tighten on my hand. He said:

"Tighten your grip."

And I tightened my grip, tightened it until my hand began to tremble. And father's hand trembled, too. I heard him say again:

"Here were ninety-nine grains of corn put up as a prize. Understand?"

Again I became confused, bewildered, and couldn't think. But in order to save father's strength I replied,

"I understand, father."

He smiled. Then he went on in a voice implying his satisfaction.

"The corn was shot from over there . . ." again father pointed at the wall, ". . . from the east. But not one of those ninety-nine grains of corn hit. Understand?"

And to save father's strength, I immediately replied,

"I understand, father."

"Good."

He coughed. He turned to the wall. After spitting out the phlegm, and wiping his lips with his hand, he went on:

"Not one hit, son. Thanks to His power. Understand?"

"Yes, father."

He paused a while and recovered his spent strength. Then he went on:

"I'm an *ulama*'s[1] son."

"Yes, father."

"But I didn't want to be a *ketib*.[2] I didn't want to be a *nalb*.[3] I didn't want to be a *penghulu*."[4] He paused for a moment. And then, "Who can tell me the day on which was born something which we'd been fighting for all this time?"

"The seventeenth of August, nineteen hundred and forty-five,[5] father."

Father smiled, pleased and content.

"Yes," he said. He felt his beard and his moustache and stroked them with his left hand.

"Would you like a shave, father?" I asked. "No."

Silence for a while.

All my brothers and sisters sat on the couch opposite father's bed.

"I didn't want to be an ulama," he continued in a firm voice. "I wanted to be a nationalist." Silence again. "That's why I became a teacher." Silence again. "To open the door for the hearts of children to go into the garden . . . ," he held it a while, "of patriotism. Are you listening?"

"Yes, father."

"Do you understand?"

"Yes, father."

"That's why I became a nationalist." Silence for a little while again. "It was hard, son." Silence again. "It really was hard to be a nationalist."

It seemed to me that his eyes sparkled a little. And I replied.

"Yes, father."

"That's why I chose to become a teacher."

"Yes, father."

"To become a pioneer of independence."

I was moved inwardly at those last words.

"But I was ready to become a nationalist. I was ready to sacrifice everything."

This time I couldn't control my feelings any longer. I tightened my grip on my father's hand and broke down and wept, wept like a little child. Father was silent at my weeping. His eyes, circled with blue, filled with tears. His stomach was convulsed. I bowed my head and let my tears fall. As I wept, I heard father's voice.

"Enough, son, don't think about it any more."

And I saw all my brothers and sisters who were sitting on the couch were crying too. And I felt in my heart: father's going to leave us. And we continued to weep. Father coughed again and then he said:

"Enough, son, enough for now. Go now, all of you. Leave me alone."

And we left father's room sobbing. I went straight to my room. I threw myself down on the couch—and thought back about everything. And I remembered vaguely the bitter letter which I had sent to him:

"It displeases me to hear news about my sister's illness. In fact I don't like it at all. Why have you, father, allowed my sister to remain ill? Men don't live just to become the victims of T.B., father. No, not by any means."

And now it came home to me that it wasn't my sister who was ill that way, but my father himself, my father himself. My heart was in turmoil. And my tears poured down. My neck became sore from my crying and finally—without realizing it—I fell asleep.

That day, too, I haven't forgotten—it was a Thursday afternoon. I woke up just before magrib. I was sitting in a chair, sipping coffee. Then my second sister, the fourth child, rushed in to find me. Falteringly she said:

"Mas, mas, father is . . . is . . . is . . . no longer with us."

Quickly, I ran to father's room, where the oil lamp was already lit. Some of my brothers and sisters were already there. I sprang quickly to father's side. I saw that his mouth was open. His hand hung limply by his side. And my wife, too, had come running and stood beside me. She said,

"Say: father!"

Because I had never been through anything like that before, I did what she said. I put my mouth to his ear and cried:

"Father!"

"Again," said my wife.

"Father!" I cried again.

Then there was a moment's silence. Suddenly I remembered father was a Muslim. And once more I put my mouth to his ear and cried:

"Allahu Akbar, Allahu Akbar, Allahu Akbar."

My sister interrupted:

"Don't let father's mouth stay open, mas."

And I closed father's jaw. I drew his eyelids down. At that moment without my being ready for it the neighbors came and helped. Father's jaw was tied with some cloth to the top of his head and then naturally—we cried together.

My sister hugged me and said plaintively in a broken voice:

"Just now, mas, just now when you were sleeping the neighbors came. Mas, they came to watch by father, mas, and father, mas, father felt unsettled. He asked them all to go, me and the others, too. And just now, mas, when . . . when I came back, mas, to give him his porridge, mas, father . . . father was already gone."

And I replied to her statement:

"Let it be, little sister. It's all over. You've still got a brother, haven't you?"

And I kissed her. But our crying was covered by the arrival of still more neighbors. And a little later—a little later our house was full of visitors.

And we were an island surrounded by those visitors.

14

That evening father's body was laid out on the couch amidst a swarm of people who sat around on chairs. There was talk about all kinds of different things. And the smoke from sweet smelling incense curled up from below the couch where the corpse was laid. The smoke was carried by the night wind, reached the nostrils of the visitors and then mixed with the smoke from cigarettes. Sometimes the sound of a person coughing could be heard—a low, hollow, painful sound—and I was startled, so were my brothers and sisters. And into our minds came a voice saying, *Has father come alive again?*

The guests gathered together in groups with friends with whom they had something in common. In one corner of the *pendopo*[1] gathered those whose conversation was about gambling.

"Oh what a shame," said a Chinese guest, "our very good friend has gone on before us. And now? Now I can't hope for *tjuk* money[2] from him again."

He was silent and looked round at his other friends.

"There wasn't anyone as determined as he was at gambling," put in another.

"Now we have to look for someone new to make up the game," another rejoined.

"Yes," said the Chinese sighing. He took a cigarette from those set out in front of him. He smoked and went on. "There wasn't anyone else who could tell stories from the history of Java so well while we were playing."

"Yes," an old man with a pot-belly took up. "And I still remember—ten years ago. There were four of us at the table. Then one of us came out with a challenge, *Come on, let's see who can stay at the cards longest.* All of us together replied, *Yes, yes. Let's.* But he was silent. All that day he didn't get up from his seat. He didn't eat. He didn't drink. That night it was the same. One by one we began to feel uneasy. The first person to get up from his place was me. And I said, I can't take it any more. I'm getting out now. And my place was taken by someone else. Then I slept for six hours. After washing and eating I went back quickly and do you know? He was still sitting in his place. People had already left two of the places and others had stepped in. And I asked, *Haven't you got up since yesterday?* He only shook his head and smiled. Five hours later I took the third place. Two days and two nights, friend, and he still hadn't moved from his place. In all he kept it up for five days and five nights. He didn't eat. He didn't drink. And he didn't even go for a pee. In my opinion he was no ordinary person."

"Like a fairy-tale," added a youngish man.

"I've also heard that story," said the Chinese, "ten years ago. But our friend isn't with us any longer." As soon as he'd stopped talking he looked into the room from the doorway to see his gambling comrade who was now laid out no longer alive.

"We're all getting old now," said the pot-belly. "It was just a month ago that my elder brother died of old age. And what about me? There's only ten years difference between me and him. We're all getting old now, aren't we?" And since nobody replied, he looked at the Chinese and went on. "And you've already got five children. And one of them's the marriageable age."

"Yes, why does life go so fast?" said the Chinese.

The man who was still quite young said:

"When he was ill I didn't get the chance to call and see him. I went to the hospital once but on the door of his room there hung a card on which was written, No visitors except for family. So I went straight back home and now, now our friend is no more." He looked into the house to see the body laid out.

"I, too, didn't visit him when he was ill," said pot-belly.

"Neither had I," said the Chinese adding his bit.

"It's a shame," said the youngish man. "When he was well we were always looking for him to make up the game. When he was ill not one of us went to see him. When he died, he died alone . . ." He fell silent as though startled by his own words. Then he went on in a voice that wasn't addressed to anyone in particular. "Yes. Why did this man have to die alone?"

Nobody replied.

And the group of gamblers thus brooded over the question put by the youngish gambler to which no one replied. That evening it was cold like most nights in the small town of Blora, which is surrounded by teak forests. Then the Chinese with his eyes on the ceiling to which there was no upper story said:

"Yes, why is it that we have to die alone? And be born alone too? And why do we have to live in a world where there are so many people? And if we're capable of loving someone and that person too loves us . . ." He went down on his knees and looked through the window into the middle of the room where the body was lying alone. He went on, "like our late friend, for example—why then do we have to be parted in death? Alone. Alone. Alone. And born alone too. Alone again. Alone again. Why wasn't this man born in the midst of the hustle and bustle of life and why didn't he die in the midst of that hustle and bustle? I'd like the world to be an all night fair."

The three friends laughed at what the Chinese had said. And the Chinese himself laughed. The others didn't understand what he had said and he himself didn't understand what he'd said. Then the conversation died. A newcomer came and sat near the group. Then someone addressed him from behind:

"Mas Mantri!"[3]

The newcomer turned round and replied:

"Oh. It's you, 'dik Djuru."

Mas Mantri sighed. Then he said very slowly:

"Our friend is dead. In my opinion we've lost a man who contributed a lot to the struggle in this area."

"Yes. He was so very active. Night and day was the same to him when it came to serving the needs of the party. But now he's dead." He sighed as if he really felt that he had lost something important in his life.

"Just think, 'dik Djuru, it was only two months ago that he came on his bike to my house to settle the business about the bonds—you know about the affair of the national bonds?"

He was silent and the man whom he called 'dik Djuru, replied,

"You mean the bonds which disappeared?"

"Yes. Those bonds were in the hands of our late friend. But the mice ran off with them to use them for their nests. Fifteen of them. But surprisingly—" he paused as if he was enjoying some beautiful memory, "he refunded the value of the bonds in full without feeling the slightest bit put out. People said that he'd sold a lot of his possessions. But I don't know for sure. It was that awareness of his responsibility which I always admired. Really! I was surprised, I admired him with all my heart. Do you know what I intended to do to him once—in the days before the war?" He was silent, waiting for a reply.

The man whom he called 'dik Djuru was silent and didn't reply. The group of card-players quietly and without being observed joined in listening to the conversation.

"When I was still mantri—long ago before the war—I received instructions from the colonial government to watch him. He was on the list as a 'red'—in the front rank. I sent three agents to tail him in turns and watch him. Do you know what he did to the tail I put on him?"

People were listening full of interest. But nobody interrupted. And Mas Mantri continued:

"One evening he knew he was being followed. He made the agent follow him into a graveyard. And because the agent didn't dare to set foot in a graveyard he waited outside the fence. One hour. Two hours. Three hours. Our friend still hadn't appeared. And the agent? He took to his heels in fright."

People laughed and the crowd of people round Mas Mantri grew larger. He told more and more stories as time went on, especially when coffee was handed round. But the night forced the guests to return each to his own home.

That night only close neighbors stayed behind. All their conversation was in praise of their friend who had just died. And without anyone noticing the new day dawned with its splendor. Fresh guests came. And visitors who hadn't closed their eyes the whole night long went to wash.

As time went by the numbers of guests increased. In the end the body, too, was taken to man's last home: the grave.

15

During the war—from the time when the Japanese landed until the collapse of Dutch authority in Indonesia—we had lost our mother and our youngest brother. The two of them lay side by side in one grave. Then beside mother's grave was the grave of grandmother. And on the other side of it was a new grave—father's last home. And beside that grave lay the grave of grandfather. Yes, we'd lost many over the war years. And the graveyard which I hadn't seen for eight years was now already full with new graves—the graves of those who were considered heroes. And among the graves of those considered heroes there were also the graves of scoundrels who because of errors in checking had been included in the company of heroes.

When the mourners had witnessed the lowering of father's body into his grave; when they had poured in their handfuls of earth; and even after father had disappeared into the embrace of the earth, I still hadn't recovered from my feelings of oppressive grief. My heart felt torn and this prevented me from thanking them as I had intended. There were several people who looked to me—because they knew I was the eldest son—to say a few words. But not one word came from my lips. Eventually they left one by one. And we—my brothers and sisters and I—went down on our knees with bowed heads in meditation over the new grave.

Oh—the man who lay buried there was the man who had given us life. Once, he, too, had had high ideals. He too had had an experience of love—a love which had failed and not failed. He had often been heard singing, singing Javanese songs, national songs and songs learned in Dutch schools. But now his voice was dead. He had been a teacher. And to thousands of students he had opened the way. He had been active in the struggle to achieve his countrymen's freedom for thirty years. And now less than a year after independence had been achieved, history had no more use for him, nor had the world, nor had mankind. And like us, too, he had experienced fear, suffering, happiness and all the other feelings there are in the human heart. But now all that was dead for him.

I wept again.

And my brothers and sisters wept again.

Then slowly we left the graveyard where the gravestones protruded. A little while ago there had been a lot of people—no less than two thousand. But now there were just us brothers and sisters. And slowly we came out onto the main road. That afternoon the burning heat began to scorch our skin. And we walked back home—to the house where mother had died, where the youngest of us had died, where father had died the day before and perhaps also where we would die one day. And on the way back home I pictured the graves of mother, my young brother, grandmother, father, and grandfather. And perhaps one day beside them my own body would be buried. And the Chinese the night before had wanted the world to be an all night fair where people came in crowds and left in crowds. There remained only those who had to sweep up what was left. And the sweeper—although he doesn't admit it himself—is the God who is constantly talked of by men who have never known him.

16

When I got back to the house all feelings of sadness, grief, and suffering disappeared. The house which from the time when I'd come from Djakarta—a month ago—had seemed dark now looked bright and shining. So did the people who lived in it. It was quiet in our house again. From the back of the house I could hear my brother who was in Form 2 in school singing the song "Old Kentucky Home." I listened in silence. But the song died away. And as though of their own accord, there came from my lips those Negro spirituals, the voice of men oppressed, the voice of men longing for something which they didn't comprehend. And the day wore on sluggishly.

The evening came on slowly. And when the sun had almost disappeared behind the western horizon there came another visitor. He said:

"I knew your late father a long time. We traveled around the country together on missions in the guerrilla area. Yes, I knew your father well. He worked for the Dutch but he kept on working for the underground. He told me a lot of things. But I don't need to tell you what he told me. I'm sure you and your brothers and sisters already know. But the only thing which I can say for certain, which perhaps you don't know, is this: your father fell on the field of politics."

I was surprised. I looked at his lips. They were still moving and I heard him say:

"I see you're surprised. But it's true that's what happened. Your father fell ill because of disappointment—he was disappointed at the state of things after independence was achieved. He felt he wasn't prepared any longer to watch the world around him degenerating—degenerating with all its consequences. Those who before had been generals in the guerrilla areas, those who had earlier held important positions before the Dutch attacked, became leaders, too, in the guerrilla areas and became real fathers of the people. And with all his energy your father supported their interests. But when independence had been achieved it was the same people who squabbled about houses and positions for themselves. And those who didn't get what they wanted, left—because they couldn't expect further payment. And your father, your father couldn't stand to see such a state of affairs. But it is in the nature of man's life that he has to mix with others. And it was the society which he had to enter which hatched your father's sickness. Your father never said anything about them. All his disappointment he simply sunk into his heart. But the outcome which was so grave and which he didn't expect happened—galloping T.B. Two and a half months he was ill and then he left us."

He paused to draw breath. And I paused to divert momentarily my attention from what he was saying. Then he sighed deeply, as if he regretted something. Then he said again:

"Perhaps what I've said is enough. Not too little, not too much. It's true your father fell on the field of politics. Your father withdrew from the party and all its trivialities in order to be able to escape from such money-grubbing clowns. But because his concern for society was so great he couldn't free himself absolutely from all of that. But you should feel proud to have had a father like him. Don't you think so?" He looked at me.

I didn't reply. I heard him sigh.

"If your father had been in a big town—and had been able to develop his true worth—perhaps he would have been someone important. Perhaps he would have been a minister." He sighed again. "But your father always held firm to the teaching of Ronggowarsito.[1] That's why he didn't want to join those clowns performing their crazy antics."

He was silent.

Twilight had come. The big drum for magrib had begun to beat incessantly. The visitor rose from his seat. He stood up and said politely and with stress:

"It's late. But don't forget this request of mine—as often as you can, put flowers on your father's grave."

Then he left. I saw him to the fence. And unexpectedly night fell fast. On this earth men aren't born into the world in swarms nor do they return to the earth in swarms. One by one they come. One by one they go. And those who have not gone anxiously await the moment when their souls will fly away to who knows where . . . .

Postscript

I began work on translating bukan pasar malam in the middle of 1970 when, newly married, I was living in a small house on the slopes of the Tunkuban Prahu in Bandung. From the window of the room in which I worked I looked out over some rice-fields. It was an ideal location and I felt very much at home in Indonesia. It was difficult to obtain Pramoedya's work in those years. The New Order was flexing its muscles, and, unless they knew you, people were reluctant to talk about what had happened in 1965–66. None of the books of the writers on the left who had been imprisoned were available in bookstores. I found this very frustrating, since I had begun to read modern Indonesian literature quite voraciously at the time, and everyone whom I asked told me that I should read the work of Pramoedya, Sitor Situmorang and others. In fact I did eventually lay my hands on their works after regularly visiting the small portable book kiosks which used to line the streets of Tjikapundung near the center of town. The booksellers there eventually got to know me and would put aside books for me, so that in time I managed to build up a reasonable collection which included not only the works of Pramoedya, but also Tan Malaka's autobiography *Dari Pendjara ke Pendjara*, his magnum opus *Madilog* and one or two other gems.

I was immediately struck by Pramoedya's novels and short stories. They were very different from the Balai Pustaka published novels of the 20s and 30s which were—and I believe still are—the staple fare of high school curricula. Those novels, for which I also have a deep affection—how could anyone fail to be thrilled by the story of Sitti Nurbaya, her lover Samsulbahri and the villainous Datuk Meringgi—were set, many of them, among the Minangkabau of West Sumatra and were redolent of another age and of a culture which was to me—at least then, before I had learned anything of the Minangkabau and their matrilineal system—remote and strange. Pramoedya's works, however, and those of his contemporaries, men like Idrus and the poet Chairil Anwar, whose poem "Aku" I learned by heart and recited to friends with great passion, were much more accessible. The experiences they described—and it must be remembered that a lot of their works, especially Pramoedya's short stories, were autobiographical—and their accounts of living through the years between 1930–1955, were graphically realistic and instantly appealing. I learned a lot about Indonesia from the literature of that period, not just about the historical events of the time but about the whole strength of cultural and political sentiment which had gone into the creation of the nation. Even in the most mundane stories there was a sense of drama, a feeling that Indonesian society of the time had been battling through a period highly-charged with emotion, strong traces of which were still to be heard in the frequently recounted reminiscences of those who had participated in the maelstrom of the times, and who could confirm for me the accuracy of the fictional descriptions and their representations of the fears and hopes, disappointments and triumphs of daily life.

Of all Pramoedya's stories the ones which most moved me were the accounts of Blora, those which appeared in the collections *Tjerita dari Blora* and *Subuh* and, above all, *Bukan PasarMalam.* Reading the last in our little house set away from the main road and looking out at the water buffalo ploughing the fields I was instantly transported by the story's narrator as he made his way home by train from Jakarta to Blora to see his dying father. The historical contextualization of the story conveyed what I liked best about Pramoedya's work, the sense of an experience which derived its power precisely from being set in a particular time in a particular place and gave the personal world of the individual a distinctive character of its own. Other people may have written about fraught journeys back to the family but none had located them in the circumstances of that critical point in Indonesia's history. For me this beautifully written novella, seemingly simple in its construction—a perfect example of *ars est celare artem*—captured exactly how it must have felt to have been alive and in Indonesia at the time. One way of trying to place that feeling is to note how a strong sense of family persists in determining the individual's orientation to the world even when there are clearly difficult tensions and profound disagreements among family members and when the events of the time have brought new and other forms of commitment and obligation to the forefront of the individual's preoccupations. If anything is characteristically Indonesian, it is this frequently uneasy disjunction between an individual's own aspirations and achievements and a continuing commitment to kin from whose outlook and circumstances he or she may feel progressively alienated but who nonetheless exercise a strong pull on his or her sense of moral obligation and personal integrity.

As soon as I had finished reading *Bukan Pasar Malam* I knew that it was something that I wanted to translate for my friends back in England who knew little of Indonesia but who would respond as I had done to the immediacy of the narrative. Translation is never an easy business and it took several attempts before I felt that I had got it right, the tone of it, not the literal meaning. When I arrived back in England after leaving that Arcadian little house, I worked a little more on the translation and sent it off to Cornell to the journal *Indonesia*. Ben Anderson was one of the editors at the time and he too shared my passion for Pramoedya's works. He read the translation and liked it, but in one or two places disagreed with my renderings. So we engaged in a long correspondence, each defending his own versions, sometimes coming to an agreement, at other times holding to his individual interpretations. Most of the time, though, I think Ben was right, and I am happy to acknowledge his help. Sometimes neither of us quite knew what was correct. We puzzled, for example, over the significance of the young narrator being addressed as Gus by a neighbor. Only much later did I learn that this was a common form of address in East Java for someone whose grandfather had been a *kiyai*, a respected religious figure in the community.

When the translation came out I was of course very pleased, but there was a sense of regret, first of all that I could not get it to Pramoedya himself and second that it would not have a larger circulation beyond the circle of specialist readers of the journal. When I was in Kuala Lumpur I tried sending a copy to Pramoedya via a friend but it never reached him. Years later in the early eighties when he had returned to Jakarta from Buru I was able to visit Pramoedya with my daughter and give him a copy of the translation. Doing this gave me a feeling of quiet satisfaction: it was a moment of a hope fulfilled, and of real pleasure at seeing Pramoedya, although not fully at liberty, at least back with his family. And now that the translation is being republished in this new form my other source of regret has disappeared. *Bukan Pasar Malam* now becomes available for a wider readership. I hope that new readers will derive as much pleasure from it as that young man of thirty years ago.

C. W. WATSON
University of Kent, Canterbury, England 2001

Notes

CHAPTER ONE

1. P . . . refers to Pesindo, a left-wing armed youth organization which joined forces with the PKI (Communist Party) at this period.
2. A *betjak* is a pedicab or a kind of trishaw in which the pedaler is at the back of the carriage.
3. Magrib: Moslem prayer performed at dusk—about 6 o'clock in Indonesia.
4. Sembah, a particular formal gesture of deference, done by placing the palms of the hands together before one's face, thumbs close to the nose, and bowing one's head slightly.

CHAPTER TWO

1. The pemuda were idealistic young militants many of whom became guerrillas and fought strenuously for the independence of Indonesia.
2. By rotten, I think, is meant the fact that his eyes are small and dull, irregularly placed, since most Indonesians find this unattractive and prefer eyes which are large and open.
3. Mas, used especially of elder brothers, is a common form of address in Central and East Java for a man older than oneself. It is commonly used by a wife addressing her husband.
4. Darul Islam was a fanatical, terrorist Muslim organization which operated in several places in Central and West Java, after independence and was not finally suppressed until 1962.

CHAPTER THREE

1. Kartini was a Javanese noblewoman (1879–1904) who campaigned for female emancipation in Indonesia by establishing educational institutes for girls. A national holiday in her honor is celebrated on April 21 every year. Pramoedya has written a two-volume biography of her entitled *Panggil Aku Kartini Sadja* (Call me simply Kartini) (Bukittinggi: Nusantara, 1962).
2. P.T.T.—Post, Telegraph and Telephone, i.e., the Central Post Office building.

CHAPTER FOUR

1. Mbak is the female equivalent of mas and is used of elder sisters.
2. Kain, a standard piece of cloth.
3. 'Dik, short for *adik,* is a form of address to younger brothers or sisters.

CHAPTER FIVE

1. Selamat, a conventional greeting of older to younger people expressing both pleasure at seeing someone and at the same time extending a blessing.

CHAPTER SIX

1. A dukun is a folk-doctor to whom various magical powers including prescience are often ascribed. It is a common practice among both the educated and the illiterate to consult a dukun—if someone is ill, or something is lost, or for similar reasons.
2. Balai Pustaka is the official state publishing house originally set up by the Dutch under the name Volkslectuur.

CHAPTER SEVEN

1. Gus, a shortened form of *agus,* is an appellation used for a small boy and, by extension, for a young man by an older person.
2. Pak is a mode of address for a man of an older generation.

3. Pasundan is West Java, the Sunda region, and is considered to be quite different from the rest of Java, hence the traditional rivalry between the Javanese and the Sundanese.

CHAPTER EIGHT

1. Sjarat is a condition or conditions which, if God wills it, will achieve a cure. A magical medicine. A regular medicine is more or less guaranteed to produce some physical improvement whereas a sjarat is not.
2. A bupati is the head of a regency. There are several regencies in a province, which is administered by a governor.
3. The rank immediately below that of bupati.

CHAPTER NINE

1. A fresh-water fish.
2. A destar is a kind of head-cloth which is wrapped around the head.

CHAPTER TEN

1. Tjendol hungkwe is a sweet drink made out of coconut milk and small cubes of tapioca.

CHAPTER THIRTEEN

1. ulama—an Islamic religious scholar.
2. ketib—the person who delivers the sermon at the service on Fridays.
3. naib—a registrar of religious affairs.
4. Penghulu—leading mosque official.
5. August 17, 1945 is the date when Independence was proclaimed.

CHAPTER FOURTEEN

1. Pendopo—a large covered area especially used for formal ceremonial occasions.

2. Tjuk—money paid by the winning gambler as "tax" to the owner of the house where the card party took place.
3. A mantri is a local civil servant whose principal duty is to see that law and order is preserved. Djuru probably is here a clerk.

CHAPTER SIXTEEN

1. Ronggowarsito was a famous nineteenth-century Javanese poet.

For more from Pramoedya Ananta Toer, look for the 

"Here is an author half a world away from us whose art and humanity are both so great that we instantly feel we've known him—and he us—all our lives." —*USA Today*

All That Is Gone

The first full-size collection of Pramoedya's short stories to appear in English, *All That Is Gone* draws from the author's own experiences in Indonesia to depict characters trying to make sense of a war-torn culture haunted by colonialism: an eight-year-old girl soon to be married off by her parents for money, an idealistic young soldier who witnesses the savage beating of a man accused of being a spy. Though violence and brutality pervade these tales, there is a profound sense of compassion present throughout—an extraordinary combination of despair and hope that gives the book rare power and beauty.

"The striking achievement of these stories is an unshakable innocence of voice and a willingness to leave judgment to the reader. Pramoedya's art is made more of sadness than of anger, and he is particularly adept at narrating from a child's perspective." —*The New Yorker* *ISBN 0-14-303446-4*

The Mute's Soliloquy: A Memoir

In 1965, Pramoedya Ananta Toer was detained by Indonesian authorities and eventually exiled to the penal island of Buru. Without a formal accusation or trial, the onetime national hero was imprisoned on Buru for eleven years. He survived under brutal conditions, somehow managing to produce his masterwork, the four novels of the Buru Quartet, as well as the remarkable journal entries, essays, and letters that comprise this moving memoir. Reminiscent of Solzhenitsyn's work, *The Mute's Soliloquy* is a harrowing portrait of a penal colony and a heartbreaking remembrance of life before it. With a resonance far beyond its particular time and place, it is a passionate tribute to the freedom of the mind and a celebration of the human spirit. *ISBN 0-14-028904-6*

The Fugitive

Written while Pramoedya Ananta Toer was imprisoned by the Dutch for his role in the Indonesian revolution after World War II, *The Fugitive* was his first major novel and the first to be published in the United States. Set during the final days of World War II, it tells the harrowing story of a young platoon leader who has led a failed nationalist revolt against Japanese forces occupying Indonesia. Betrayed by a coconspirator and forced to disguise himself as a beggar, he sets out to find his fiancée while eluding the military forces that will kill him if they capture him. Combining acute political and social criticism with a gripping, deeply moving narrative, this timeless story of a soldier's return home will haunt anyone who reads it. *ISBN 0-14-029652-2*

THE BURU QUARTET

This Earth of Mankind

With *This Earth of Mankind* comes the first chapter of Pramoedya Ananta Toer's epic quartet, set in the Dutch East Indies at the turn of the century, immersing the reader in an astonishingly vivid world. Living equally among the colonists and colonized of nineteenth-century Java, Minke is a young Javanese student of great intelligence and ambition. Battling against the confines of colonial strictures, it is his love for Annelies that enables him to find the strength to embrace his world. *ISBN 0-14-025635-0*

Child of All Nations

In *Child of All Nations*, the reader is immediately swept up by a story that is profoundly feminist, devastatingly anticolonialist, and full of heartbreak, suspense, love, and fury: the cultural whirlpool that was the Dutch East Indies of the 1890s. A story of awakening, it follows Minke, the main character of *This Earth of Mankind*, as he struggles to overcome the injustice all around him. Pramoedya's full literary genius is evident in the brilliant characters that populate this world: Minke's fragile mixed-race wife; a young Chinese revolutionary; an embattled Javanese peasant and his impoverished family; and the French painter Jean Marais, to name just a few. *ISBN 0-14-025633-4*

Footsteps

As the world moves into the twentieth century, Minke, one of the few European-educated Javanese, optimistically starts a new life in a new town. With his enrollment in medical school and the opportunity to meet people, there is every reason to believe that he can leave behind the tragedies of the past. But as his world begins to fall apart, Minke draws a small but fervent group around him to fight back against colonial exploitation. During the struggle, Minke finds love, friendship, and betrayal—with tragic consequences. And he goes from wanting to understand his world to wanting to change it. Pramoedya's genius is again evident in his depiction of a people's painful emergence from colonial domination and the shackles of tradition. *ISBN 0-14-025634-2*

House of Glass

A novel of heroism, passion, and betrayal, *House of Glass* provides a spectacular conclusion to a series hailed as one of the great works of modern literature. Minke, writer and leader of the dissident movement, is now imprisoned and the narrative has switched to Pangemanann, a former policeman, who has the task of spying and reporting on those who continue the struggle for independence. But Pangemanann is a victim of his own conscience and must decide whether the law is to control or safeguard the rights of the people. At last Pangemanann sees that his true opponents are not Minke and his followers, but rather the dynamism and energy of a society awakened.

ISBN 0-14-025679-2

Printed in the United States
by Baker & Taylor Publisher Services